W9-DBM-454

# LITTLE HOUSE IN THE CLASSROOM

### by
### Christine Olivieri Hackett

### illustrated by Vanessa Filkins

Cover by Vanessa Filkins

Copyright © Good Apple, Inc., 1989

ISBN No. 0-86653-444-X

Printing No. 987654321

**GOOD APPLE, INC.**
**BOX 299**
**CARTHAGE, IL 62321**

The purchase of this book entitles the buyer to reproduce student activity pages for classroom use only. Any other use requires written permission from Good Apple, Inc.

All rights reserved. Printed in the United States of America.

# TABLE OF CONTENTS

# DEDICATION

To G.P.H.
For the idea,
    the travel,
    the patience,
    and the support.
But most of all . . .
    for Eternity.

C.O.H.

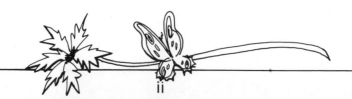

Copyright © 1989, Good Apple, Inc.

GA1052

# INTRODUCTION

Laura Ingalls Wilder wrote a total of nine books, seven of which are used here. Not included are *Farmer Boy*, which deals with Laura's husband Almanzo, and *The First Four Years*, which delves into the first years of Laura and Almanzo's marriage. A separate unit is devoted to each of the seven books with activities in music, art, cooking, writing, reading and math. Also included are bulletin board and learning center ideas as well as games.

The purpose of these units is (1) to incorporate children's literature into the everyday curriculum of the classroom; (2) to make children aware of the past; (3) to use storybooks as lessons; (4) to show students by using different media what things "used to be" before television, grocery stores and McDonald's. The goal of these units is to provide teachers with a guide to refer to in step-by-step format when using Mrs. Wilder's books. The reader will notice that several chapters have more than one activity. All need not be done. These are only suggestions. They are designed to be used as an entire unit that covers many subject areas, but no activity is dependent upon the prior use of any other. Also included is a summary of each book and a list of skills utilized in each unit.

It is the author's hope to have provided a supplemental resource in children's literature which will be of value to both the teacher and the student.

Copyright © 1989, Good Apple, Inc.

GA1052

# BACKGROUND INFORMATION ON LAURA AND HER FAMILY

Laura Ingalls Wilder was the dynamic, sensitive writer of some of America's best loved children's literature—the "Little House" books. Born February 7, 1867, Laura Elizabeth Ingalls began her life in the Big Woods of Pepin County, Wisconsin. It is in these Big Woods Laura begins telling of her growing-up years. Her stories are told through a child's eyes but appeal to adults as well.

Laura Ingalls Wilder lived a full, rich life and her books have brought much happiness to both children and adults. She was the author of nine books, the first of which—*Little House in the Big Woods*—was published in 1932. The eight books that followed were as well-loved as the first.

Copyright © 1989, Good Apple, Inc.

2

GA1052

# LOST YEARS FOR LAURA

Laura was the second daughter born to Pa and Ma Ingalls in Pepin County, Wisconsin, more commonly known as the Big Woods. Their first daughter, Mary Amelia, was born January 10, 1865, and shared her birthday with Pa.

Laura was barely one year old when Pa decided to move to Kansas where acres of new farmland were for sale to settlers. So move they did into Indian Territory—Rutland Township, Montgomery County, Kansas. It is here in Kansas the book, *Little House on the Prairie*, takes place. But, as stated above, these were lost years for Laura; she was too young to remember.

When Laura was four years old, the wagon was packed again, and Pa, Ma, Mary, Laura and a new little sister named Carolina Celestia (Carrie, born August 3, 1870) after Ma, were going *back* to Pepin County, Wisconsin—the Big Woods. Only now, Laura *was* old enough to remember!

# LAURA'S BIG WOODS

The Big Woods that Laura remembered are vividly described in *Little House in the Big Woods*. However, Laura did leave out some information about her life that occurred during those years.

Since there were no laws, or effective ones, there were men who would steal and murder. These things occurred frequently not far from Laura's house. Such incidents she did not describe in her books.

Another event in Laura's life in the Big Woods was school. At the tender age of four, Laura, along with Mary, attended Berry Corner School, named after its location. Laura, however, did not attend as many terms as Mary.

Copyright © 1989, Good Apple, Inc.

GA1052

Laura's adventures in the Big Woods again, however, did not last more than a few years. In October of 1873, Pa and Ma sold their land in Wisconsin. The Ingalls again were on their way west.

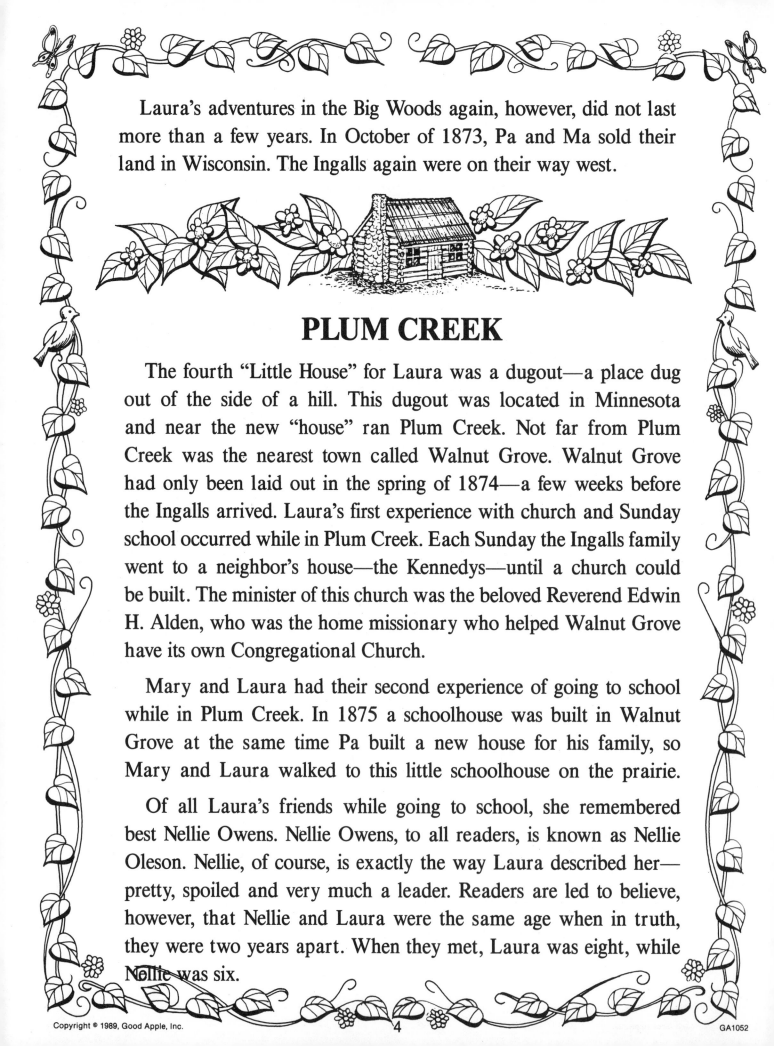

# PLUM CREEK

The fourth "Little House" for Laura was a dugout—a place dug out of the side of a hill. This dugout was located in Minnesota and near the new "house" ran Plum Creek. Not far from Plum Creek was the nearest town called Walnut Grove. Walnut Grove had only been laid out in the spring of 1874—a few weeks before the Ingalls arrived. Laura's first experience with church and Sunday school occurred while in Plum Creek. Each Sunday the Ingalls family went to a neighbor's house—the Kennedys—until a church could be built. The minister of this church was the beloved Reverend Edwin H. Alden, who was the home missionary who helped Walnut Grove have its own Congregational Church.

Mary and Laura had their second experience of going to school while in Plum Creek. In 1875 a schoolhouse was built in Walnut Grove at the same time Pa built a new house for his family, so Mary and Laura walked to this little schoolhouse on the prairie.

Of all Laura's friends while going to school, she remembered best Nellie Owens. Nellie Owens, to all readers, is known as Nellie Oleson. Nellie, of course, is exactly the way Laura described her—pretty, spoiled and very much a leader. Readers are led to believe, however, that Nellie and Laura were the same age when in truth, they were two years apart. When they met, Laura was eight, while Nellie was six.

Copyright © 1989, Good Apple, Inc.

4

GA1052

The Ingalls family seemed to be getting along rather well on Plum Creek by this time. Laura and Mary were attending school, and Pa's crop of wheat was doing well. One week before the harvest, however, the sunlight seemed to disappear; the grasshoppers had come.

As was true of most settlers, Pa's crop was lost. He, like others, decided to travel east where the grasshoppers had not done damage.

In the fall of 1875, Ma, Pa, Mary, Laura, and Carrie moved to a house in Walnut Grove—Ma was expecting a baby. On November 1, 1875, Ma delivered a new baby to her family, a boy who was named Charles Fredrick Ingalls.

Even though there was a new baby in the Ingalls' home, times seemed worse than ever. People were leaving Plum Creek; no one wanted to risk another season of grasshoppers. The Ingalls, too, decided not to stay. They were going East again—to Minnesota where aunts and uncles of Laura were.

# THE GAP IN LAURA'S BOOKS

Time lapsed between the books *On the Banks of Plum Creek* and *By the Shores of Silver Lake*. Suddenly, the Ingalls were moving and Mary became blind. What happened during those missing years? Why had Laura not written about them? The truth is, the Ingalls suffered many, many hardships after the grasshoppers had destroyed Pa's wheat crop. It seemed going back East was the only hope.

Copyright © 1989, Good Apple, Inc.

5

Laura was nine years old, Mary was eleven and Carrie six when the Ingalls set out for Uncle Peter's house. It was here they were going to stay only a little while, however. They were on their way to a place called Burr Oak, Iowa. Pa had a friend, Mr. Steadman, who had traded for a hotel in Burr Oak. Mr. Steadman had asked Pa and Ma to be partners, so in the fall of that year the Ingalls would move on.

Before Ma, Pa, the girls and baby Freddie were to reach Burr Oak, Iowa, they were to stay awhile with Pa's brother whom Laura knew as Uncle Peter.

To Laura, life at Uncle Peter's was a happy time. After all, at the tender age of nine what child could not be happy? But by August of 1876, Pa and Ma were very unhappy, for baby Freddie was very ill. It seemed no doctor could do anything to make Freddie better. Charles Fredrick Ingalls, age nine months, died on Sunday, August 27, 1876.

At Laura's age, she now knew how hard pioneer life could be. As she grew older, she never wrote of the hard days she and her family encountered on the way to Burr Oak.

Burr Oak lies in the hills of northeastern Iowa. It was not a new town like the ones Laura was used to, but this was her new home.

The Ingalls came to Iowa to be partners with the Steadman family, also formerly of Walnut Grove, to run the Burr Oak House, a hotel, formerly called Masters Hotel. Burr Oak House was one of two hotels in the town; the other was The American House. Both hotels were dependent on travelers for their livelihood, thus at various times were troubled financially.

Copyright © 1989, Good Apple, Inc.

GA1052

The Ingalls lived in the Burr Oak House. The one thing that bothered Pa and Ma about living in this hotel was that there was a barroom where men drank and were at times boisterous. Needless to say, however, here the Ingalls must stay. Not only were Pa and Ma helping to run the hotel, but Pa took a job with a man named J.H. Porter, who ran a grinding mill. Laura and Mary also had various jobs to do at the hotel. When they were not in school, they waited on tables or washed dishes.

Christmastime at the Masters Hotel was quite a disappointment for Laura. Christmas had always been such a joy in the Ingalls' home, and every one of Mrs. Wilder's books contains at least one joyous chapter of the occasion.

The Ingalls family lived in Burr Oak Hotel for only a short time. In January 1877, Pa moved his family to rooms above a grocery store which was next door to the hotel. This little house was short lived, too. Several happenings at a nearby saloon forced Pa to move again, and rightfully so, for Ma was expecting a baby soon.

The next little house for Laura was a little red brick owned by a man named Mr. Bisby, who lived in Burr Oak Hotel. While living here, Laura continued her schooling, and on May 23, 1877, she had a new sister named Grace. It is said the name Grace was chosen because Ma and Pa felt she was a special gift to replace little Freddie.

The summer of 1877 was a wonderful summer for Laura, but by summer's end she saw that Pa was restless. He had worked so hard for so little and was in deep debt. Perhaps, she alone had enjoyed the summer. Perhaps, again for the Ingalls, it was a time to pack the wagon and move on.

Copyright © 1989, Good Apple, Inc.

GA1052

# BACK TO WALNUT GROVE

In a time that spanned a little over a year, Pa, Ma, and their four girls were moving back to Walnut Grove, Minnesota. Laura was ten years old, going on eleven. She knew hard times as well as good times, and she realized going back into grasshopper country would still bring more hard times.

Little had changed from the time Laura left Walnut Grove. Most of her friends were still there, and Mary and Laura returned to school with them. Laura's favorite subject in school was spelling, and the best part of spelling was the spelling bees. Not only were spelling bees held in school, but every Friday night a spelling bee was held in the schoolhouse for parents to see their children spell.

Until the spring, the Ingalls lived with the Ensign family in their home. Pa had taken a job with a man named Mr. Masters and worked for him in a hotel in Walnut Grove. By the time spring rolled around, Pa had saved enough money to build a small house for his family. At this time Pa rented a room in town and opened a butcher shop. Laura also took a job at this time. She was eleven years old and worked for Emeline Masters in the hotel; she was paid fifty cents a day.

It is true that Laura was truly enjoying this time in her life, but all was not well with Pa and Ma. Money was scarce and as always Pa's eye was looking west. Tragedy again struck the Ingalls family in the spring of 1879; Laura was twelve years old. Mary was suddenly very ill with a fever. As a result of her illness, she lost her sight in both eyes.

Copyright © 1989, Good Apple, Inc.

GA1052

# MOVING WEST AGAIN

When things seemed at their worst for the Ingalls family, an unexpected visit from Laura's Aunt Docia brought a ray of hope. It seemed Aunt Docia's husband Hiram—Uncle Hi—was working as a contractor on the railroad in the West. Uncle Hi was in need of a storekeeper, bookkeeper and timekeeper. The job paid fifty dollars a month, and she was offering it to Pa. Pa was delighted, but Ma did not want to leave the settled country. But for every reason Ma had for staying, Pa found another for leaving. The Ingalls were going west—to Dakota Territory.

Pa left soon after Aunt Docia's visit while Ma and the girls came out West on the train a few months later. After they arrived in Tracy (as far as the train went), Pa picked up his family in the wagon and their trip to Dakota Territory began. For a short while, the Ingalls stayed at Aunt Docia's at Big Sioux railroad camp; then it was a trip of thirty-five miles to Silver Lake Camp. While at Silver Lake Camp, home was a small shanty.

The Ingalls' stay was short-lived, however, for in early December the camp began to clear out leaving only a few people. But Pa liked Silver Lake. He once told Ma before leaving Walnut Grove, if she would agree to go west, it would be the last move he ever made; he would wander no more. This promise he intended to keep here at Silver Lake in Dakota Territory.

By the time Laura reached her thirteenth birthday in February of 1880, the Ingalls were snug in the surveyor's house. Pa had made a deal with the railroad men to keep an eye on the railroad property, and in return Pa and his family would live in their house.

All the pain that had gone before seemed to ease for the Ingalls during their stay in the surveyor's house. The house was small but cozy which was so true of all the Ingalls' homes. There were new friends, too—Mr. and Mrs. Robert Boast who became life-long friends of the Ingalls.

Copyright © 1989, Good Apple, Inc.

9

GA1052

Along with springtime came a rush of new settlers in the new town of De Smet, Dakota Territory, located near Silver Lake. For a long time, Pa and Ma took in travellers so they would have a place to spend the night. But soon Pa built a store in the new town and he moved his family in. For Laura, living in town was more of a dread than a joy. There were too many people, too much noise. She was anxious to move to the homestead claim Pa purchased southeast of town.

Life on the claim as it turned out was not going to be the land of plenty. The sun raged hot through the summer months, more and more people moved in, hunting became poor and Pa's eye was looking west to Oregon. But he had made a promise to Ma—one he never broke—and kept struggling on.

There was an unexpected blizzard in Dakota Territory in October of 1880 which forced the Ingalls to move back to Pa's storehouse in town. Laura was not happy, since she did not like town, but being there held one advantage—she could go to school (she had not attended for over a year)! Laura made a few life-long friends upon returning—Mary Power, Minne Johnson, Cap Garland and Ben Woodworth. Laura enjoyed school—it made living in town bearable, but her enjoyment was short-lived. What came to be known for years after as the "Hard Winter" began towards the end of November 1880. Blizzards came without warning after that, one after another. School was shut down until the winter winds died down. Since blizzards struck so suddenly and continuously, trains were not able to get through. From January 1881 until May, De Smet was alone on the prairie to fend for itself. The Ingalls family got along as best they could though fuel was low and meals were kept small. It was not until May of 1881 that De Smet found relief when the snowed-in trains were able to bring food and supplies to the starving town.

Copyright © 1989, Good Apple, Inc.

# THESE HAPPY GOLDEN YEARS

In the year 1881, Mary was sixteen years old, Laura fourteen, going on fifteen, and Carrie was eleven. The hard winter was over, but it had left its mark on all the townspeople. Laura, however, was about to embark on another new adventure—a job in town! She was to work in Mr. Clayton's dry goods store for Martha White, sewing and basting men's shirts. Laura's feelings had not changed toward town; she still did not like it. But she knew she must overcome her dread, for the money she earned would help send Mary to the school for the blind. The school Mary was to attend was in Vinton, Iowa, and Pa and Ma took her there in the fall of 1881.

In the winter of 1881, Pa moved his family back to town and Laura, along with Carrie, began to attend school. Upon returning, she became reacquainted with her old friends and acquired some new ones as well. To Laura's surprise, one of the new faces belonged to a girl named Genny Masters. Laura had met Genny in Walnut Grove and likened her to Nellie Owens. Readers should note here that Mrs. Wilder tells of Nellie Oleson's return to school, when in actuality, Genny Masters was the girl Laura described in *Little Town on the Prairie.*

The town of De Smet was growing with leaps and bounds! Townspeople gathered together for sociables and various other pleasures. At this time Laura was asked for her first date. The boy's name was Alfred Thomas, a young lawyer, but quite by mistake Laura said no. The next boy to ask her out was Ernie Perry— and to be sure, she said yes.

Copyright © 1989, Good Apple, Inc.

GA1052

In the summer of 1882 on the prairie Laura loved so very much, she was busy studying her books. She was preparing to be a teacher, something she dreaded terribly, but must do because the money would help keep Mary in the School for the Blind. Prayer meetings and revivals also made their way to De Smet that year, and reluctantly Laura attended. It was during this time that Almanzo Wilder began escorting Laura home. Laura knew little about Almanzo—after all, he was ten years older than she and was already a homesteader. The one thing Laura was sure of was that Almanzo had two beautiful Morgan horses that Laura hoped she might ride behind.

It was said that in order to get a teacher's certificate, one must be sixteen years of age. One day in early December, Mr. Boast came by the Ingalls with a man named Louis Bouchie. Mr. Bouchie lived twelve miles south of De Smet where an abandoned claim shanty was turned into a schoolhouse. They needed a teacher for the school and Mr. Boast recommended Laura. After taking her teachers' examination, on December 10, 1883, Laura received her teaching certificate at the age of fifteen and then, with her parents' blessing, accepted Mr. Bouchie's offer.

Bouchie School (to readers known as Brewster School) was far enough from De Smet that Laura had to live with Mr. and Mrs. Bouchie and their small son Johnnie. Because of Mrs. Bouchie's unfriendliness, Laura saw she was not welcome. She kept remembering, however, that only two months must pass and she would be gone from that dreadful house.

Much to Laura's surprise though, Almanzo Wilder made the long twelve-mile trip to Bouchie School every Friday to take Laura home for the weekend. On Sunday then, he brought her back for another week at school. Those weekends at home helped her endure the Bouchie household throughout the week.

Copyright © 1989, Good Apple, Inc.

GA1052

When Bouchie School was over, Laura had turned sixteen. She now had a job on Saturday helping a dressmaker. Her life was happy and she began to think of Almanzo as more than a friend. Mary came home in June of that year and Laura enjoyed her summer. By the time Mary left in September though, Laura's thoughts were still on Almanzo. Almanzo, too, had Laura on his mind and once again they began their weekly Sunday drives together in his buggy.

As Laura and Almanzo began their romance, they both enjoyed the social events of town life. Laura was growing up, and the one thing she loved about town—school—was suddenly boring. Laura was not a little girl anymore; by the end of summer she was an engaged young woman.

The next year of Laura's life was not especially exciting. She and Almanzo took their Sunday drives, and Laura taught school until the term's end in July. Laura and Almanzo had planned to marry in the fall of 1885, but an interfering sister—Eliza Jane Wilder—had other ideas; she wanted a big wedding. To avoid any family complications, Laura and Almanzo were quietly married on August 25, 1885, by Reverend Brown.

# SORROWS AND JOYS

The first years of Laura and Almanzo's marriage were far from joyous. Those first four years were overshadowed by sorrow.

The first year brought one joy to the Wilder family though—Laura was pregnant. On December 5, 1886, Laura gave birth to a daughter whom she named Rose. Rose was named after the prairie flowers Laura had always loved. But Laura was not truly happy. In reality, she was not sure she wanted to be a farmer's wife. A farmer was tied down and Laura wanted to be free; a farmer had constant debts—which was true of Almanzo as well. Laura worried most of the time about the lack of money.

Copyright © 1989, Good Apple, Inc.

In the summer of 1887, a fire destroyed the barn and haystacks. The next spring both Laura and Almanzo suffered from diphtheria; and Almanzo suffered a stroke, which left him shuffling as he walked and forced the use of a cane. Laura gave birth to a son in 1889, a naturally joyous event, but the baby died twelve days later. On August 23, 1889, the kitchen of their little gray house burned down. By the spring of 1890, they left Dakota; there was no hope or reason to stay. They stopped awhile at the farm of Almanzo's parents before reaching their destination—Florida. They were gone two years, but happiness was still not to be found. The Wilders headed back to Dakota.

Pa and Ma now lived in a house in town. Mary was home from college, Carrie was twenty-two and working, and Grace at fifteen was enjoying her school days. Laura, Almanzo and Rose joined Pa and Ma in town where they rented a house. During this time Laura took a job with a dressmaker and Almanzo did odd jobs. Eventually, Laura began to save money.

In July 1894, the Wilders packed their belongings once and left for new and unfound dreams. The wagon stopped at Mansfield, Missouri, in the Ozarks; this was home. Laura and Almanzo bought forty acres of land which was very, very rocky. In a few years their acreage increased to two hundred and acquired the name Rocky Ridge Farm.

Laura and Almanzo's life together had prospered. They were not the shy hopeful couple of years past. They had grown in love by helping each other and now their lives were full of joy. In the spring of 1902, Laura received news from far-off Dakota—Pa was ill. Laura, alone, went home to the prairie she so dearly loved and arrived just before Pa's death on June 8, 1902.

Copyright © 1989, Good Apple, Inc.

GA1052

At the age of thirty-five, she was at last happy and content as a farmer's wife. To Almanzo and Laura's delight, Rose was making quite a name for herself. In the summer of 1902, she went to Louisiana with her Aunt Eliza Jane Wilder where she attended school. Rose became a telegrapher, a business woman in California, a newswriter and correspondent; she traveled worldwide making her parents very proud.

In the year 1924, Laura was again saddened by the loss of Ma, who died at eighty-five years old. Carrie was married and had moved to the Black Hills; Grace, too, married but stayed close to home. Laura, nearing sixty, had a rich life. She wrote articles for newspapers in Missouri on farm life and at times about her childhood. Her life as a pioneer girl had not died.

In 1930, Laura was sixty-three years old, and Almanzo was seventy-three. Ma and Pa were gone and Mary had died in 1928. Still her memory of her childhood days burned inside her. So she wrote. She wrote of Pa and Ma, of Cap Garland and Nellie Oleson. She brought to life her childhood—she created the "Little House" books. *Little House in the Big Woods* was published in 1932; *Farmer Boy*, in 1932; *Little House on the Prairie*, 1935, *On the Banks of Plum Creek*, 1937; *By the Shores of Silver Lake*, 1939; *The Long Winter*, 1940; *Little Town on the Prairie*, 1941; and *These Happy Golden Years*, 1943.

Laura was happy. In 1939, after the manuscript for *By the Shores of Silver Lake* was complete, the Wilders went home to De Smet one last time. To the "Land of Used-to-be" they traveled in their Chrysler. They saw Carrie and Grace and many old friends. They had one final glimpse of yesteryear.

Copyright © 1989, Good Apple, Inc.
GA1052

Two years after their visit to De Smet, Grace died and in 1946 Carrie too was gone. Laura was now the only member left of her pioneering family. Three years later Almanzo suffered a heart attack at the age of ninety-two. Though fight he did, he died in October of 1949.

Laura was deeply saddened, but one joy sustained her. She found constant delight to think her stories were so loved by children everywhere. She received a constant flow of letters from readers telling how much they loved her books and her. Laura was happy, but alone too. She was tired when she reached her ninetieth birthday on February 7, 1957. Laura remembered her days of being a schoolgirl, of Mary, of Pa.

> When the fiddle had stopped singing Laura called out softly, "What are days of auld lang syne, Pa?" "They are the days of a long time ago, Laura," Pa said. "Go to sleep, now." But Laura lay awake a little while listening to Pa's fiddle softly playing and to the lonely sound of the wind in the Big Woods. She looked at Pa sitting on the bench by the hearth, the firelight gleaming on the honey-brown fiddle. She looked at Ma, gently rocking and knitting. She thought to herself, "This is now." She was glad that the cozy house, and Pa and Ma and the firelight and the music, were now. They could not be forgotten, she thought, because now is now. It can never be a long time ago.[1]

Laura Ingalls Wilder died February 10, 1957, at the age of ninety.

[1]Donald Zochert, *Laura, the Life of Laura Ingalls Wilder* (Chicago: Regnery Company, 1976), p. i.

Copyright © 1989, Good Apple, Inc. GA1052

# UNIT 1
# LITTLE HOUSE IN THE
# BIG WOODS

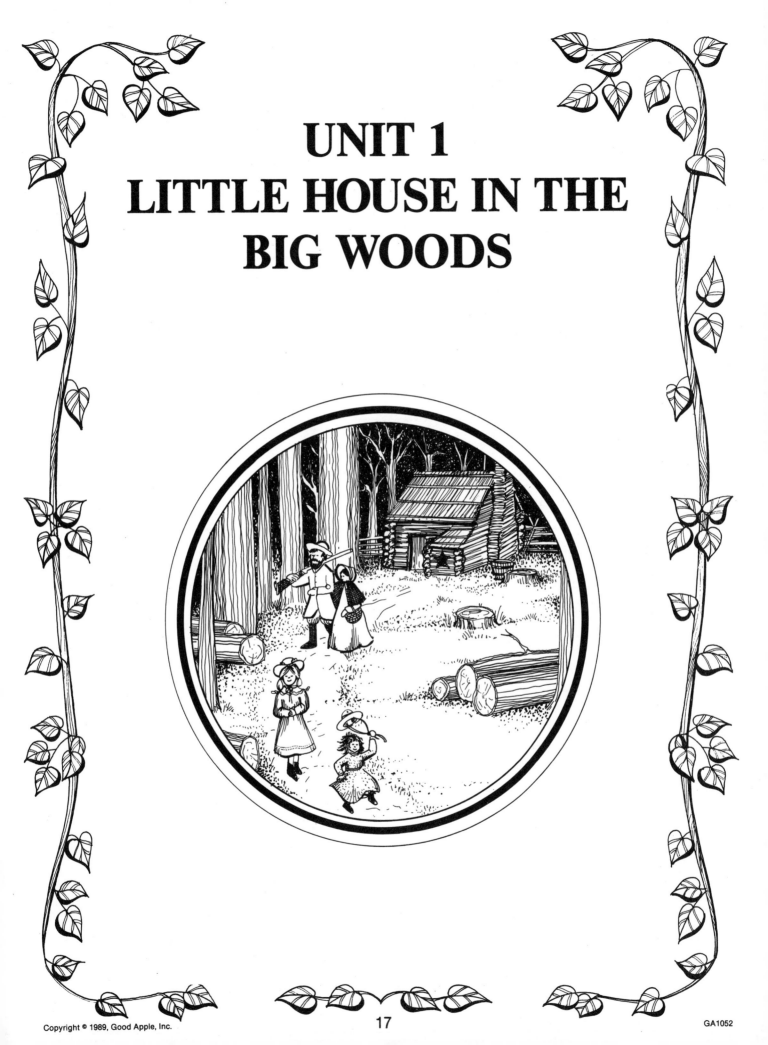

Copyright © 1989, Good Apple, Inc.

# UNIT 1

| SKILL | CHAPTER |
|-------|---------|
| Critical Thinking | 1, 2, 3, 6 |
| Writing Activities | 2, 7 |
| Oral and Listening Skills | Entire |
| Bulletin Board Ideas | 1, 2, 3, 6 |
| Art | 1, 3, 5, 6 |
| Social Studies | 1, 3, 7 |
| Science | 7 |
| Math | 2, 4, 5, 8 |
| Guidance | 10 |
| Setting the Stage for Reading | 1, 3, 4 |
| Comprehensive Skills | Work Sheet |
| Study Skills | Work Sheet |

Copyright © 1989, Good Apple, Inc.

GA1052

# UNIT 1

# LITTLE HOUSE IN THE BIG WOODS

The "Big Woods"—the place of Laura's birth and the beginnings of a very enchanting childhood are revealed in Mrs. Wilder's first book.

*Little House in the Big Woods* portrays a little girl with eyes full of wonder and a heart full of love for her Ma and Pa and sister Mary. The theme of this book is very clear and simple—caring, sharing and growing up during a time when, even though you are a little girl, you do your part to help your family. The theme is brought out simply in each chapter. Laura and Mary had their "chores" each and every day. They were done—without hesitation or pushing from Ma and Pa—completely and thoroughly; then and only then would Laura play.

*Little House in the Big Woods* is one adventure after another in Laura's life. It's a book of vivid descriptions of first-time happenings for Laura. There's the dance at Grandpa's where Laura watches all the "big girls" dress up. There is Laura's first experience at seeing a town, and of course the fun at butchering time roasting the pig's tail!

Copyright © 1989, Good Apple, Inc.

GA1052

# CHAPTER 1

- Show a map of Wisconsin. Locate Pepin County. A reproducible map is found on page 21 of this book.

- Show a map of the United States. Have students compare the state of Wisconsin with their own state.

- Reproduce the map of the United States on page 22 in this book for each student. Instruct students to locate the state of Wisconsin on their outline maps and color it blue. As the Ingalls family travels from state to state, students will find each state on their maps and color it. Students should fold maps in half and place in the front of their social studies book for safekeeping. Instruct children to color in the state in which they live to visually see the relationship to where the Ingalls lived.

- Before reading, show several pictures of things the class will hear about in this chapter. Example: wolves, muskrats, mink, otter, foxes, deer, trundle beds, smokehouses made from logs and described on page 6 and shown on page 8, corncob doll named "Susan" and Pa's traps.

- Read Chapter 1 on the first day, referring to previously shown pictures or examples.

- After reading the entire chapter, follow up with some comprehension questions.

  a. What kinds of food did Laura and her family eat?

  b. Name the members of Laura's family.

  You may wish to write answers on the board.

Copyright © 1989, Good Apple, Inc.

GA1052

# WISCONSIN

**Pepin County**

Copyright © 1989, Good Apple, Inc.

21

GA1052

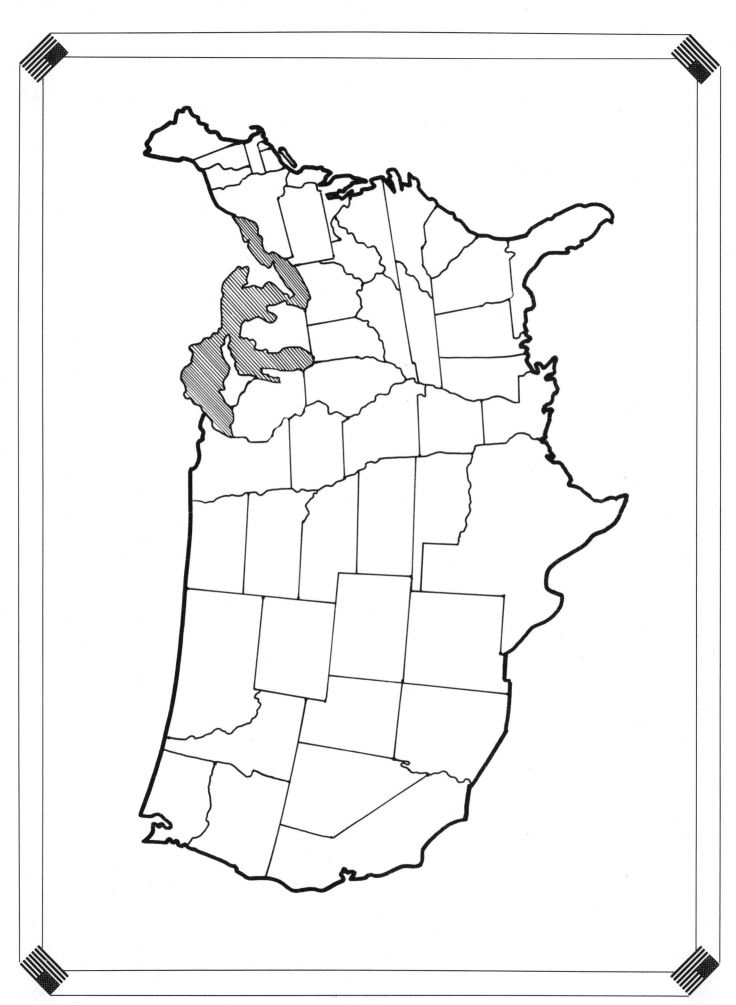

Copyright © 1989, Good Apple, Inc.

22

GA1052

## CHAPTER 1 (cont'd.)

● The following art activity can serve as a culmination to chapter 1.

> "Laura lived in the big, big woods of Wisconsin with her Ma, Pa and two sisters, Mary and Carrie. What do you think her house looked like?"

Using the log cabin pattern provided, copy a log cabin for each student. Ask students to draw the inside of the house on one side and the outside on the other.

Display the finished log cabins by hanging them from the light fixtures while *Little House in the Big Woods* is being read.

Copyright © 1989, Good Apple, Inc.

GA1052

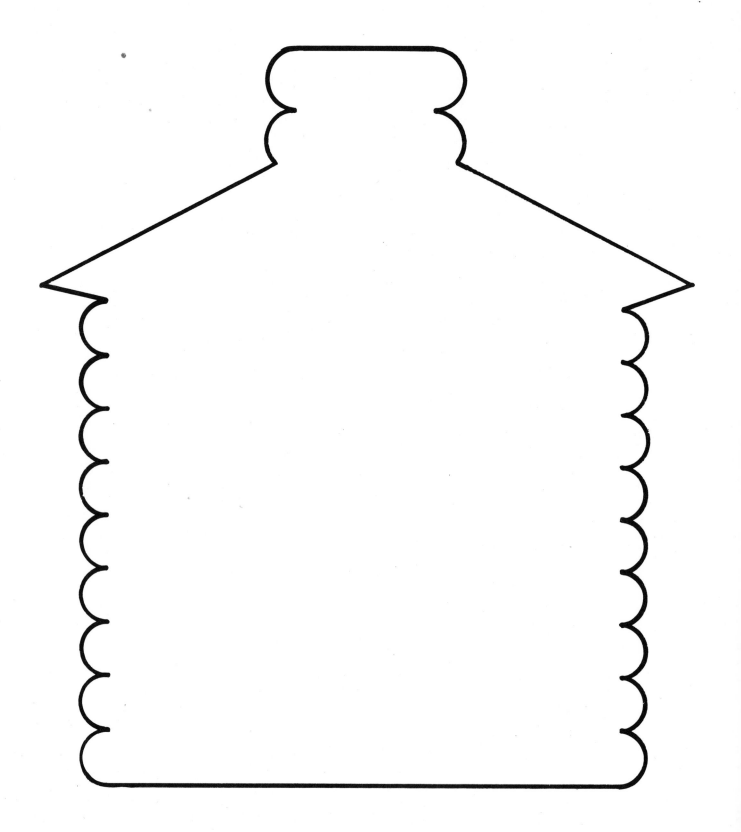

Copyright © 1989, Good Apple, Inc.

24

GA1052

# CHAPTER 2

- Ask the following review questions on Chapter 1:

  a. Name the members of the Ingalls family.
  b. Where did Pa get the food for his family?
  c. What was the smokehouse used for?
  d. Where did Laura and her family live?

- Read Chapter 2 in its entirety. There are three activities in this chapter. Each activity may require several days to complete.

## MY FAVORITE DAY

On page 29, Ma quoted a verse for a chore relating to each day of the week. Write the verse on the board and have the class read aloud each line. Ask children to think about their own favorite day and reason for their preference. Reproduce My Favorite Day activity sheet and instruct them to explain in writing their favorite day; then draw a picture at the bottom that illustrates that day. These finished projects can serve as a bulletin board of both creative writing and excellent penmanship!

## MAKING BUTTER

The topic of food appears many times throughout the Laura Ingalls Wilder books. As an introduction to cooking, making butter like Ma, Mary and Laura did can be great fun for your class.

The process is described on pages 168-169 of *The Little House Cookbook: Frontier Foods from Laura Ingalls Wilder's Classic Stories* by Barbara M. Walker (New York: Harper & Row, 1979), or use the method described on the following page.

Copyright © 1989, Good Apple, Inc.

GA1052

## CHAPTER 2 (cont'd.)

1. Have each student bring a small jar from home.
2. Fill each jar ¼ to ½ full with heavy whipping cream provided by the teacher.
3. Students shake jars vigorously.
4. Cream will separate, leaving a lump of butter.
5. Refrigerate and eat with crackers, later in the day.
6. While the class is enjoying their homemade butter, discuss how this process is different from making butter today.

## JACK FROST ART

You will need granulated sugar and a set of measuring cups for this activity. Have each student bring a shoe box lid from home. Student places a cup of sugar in box lid. With his fingers, he makes a picture like "Jack Frost" made on pages 26 and 27.

Copyright © 1989, Good Apple, Inc.

GA1052

# My Favorite Day

Copyright © 1989, Good Apple, Inc.

GA1052

# CHAPTER 3

- Ask these questions to review Chapter 2.
  a. Ma had a poem for every day of the work week. Who can remember what she said?
  b. How did Ma make the butter turn a yellowish color?
  c. Did Ma use a churn to make her butter?

- Begin this chapter by showing pictures of old guns that were used in Pa's day. Also show pictures of bullets, a bullet pouch, ramrod, and a cowhorn.

- Read "The Story of Pa and the Voice in the Woods" (pages 53-58) in its entirety without interruption.

  Upon reaching the last paragraph on page 58, ask this question: "What scared Pa?" Discuss with children all possibilities and list their responses on the board. Students should defend their suggestions.

- At the conclusion of this discussion, read the last sentence from the story that spells out the correct answer. Then assign the following art activity.

## PA'S SURPRISE

### BULLETIN BOARD

SUPPLIES:
  lunch bags
  newspaper
  crayons

STUDENT DIRECTIONS:
  Place lunch bag on your desk, flap side down. With your crayons, decorate bag with feathers, eyes and beak. Open the bag and stuff almost full of crumpled newspaper. Close unstuffed bottom off by tying with string.

Copyright © 1989, Good Apple, Inc.

GA1052

# CHAPTER 3 (cont'd.)

TEACHER DIRECTIONS:

Do each of the steps with the students. Be sure to offer assistance with the string. Make a large tree with lots of branches. Place owls on branches by tucking string and "tails" under branches and staple. This makes a great bulletin board for October.

Discuss how the Ingalls family could not live without their "environment" and how they depended on it for their food and livelihood just as many of our great-grandparents and perhaps grandparents did.

Copyright © 1989, Good Apple, Inc.

GA1052

# CHAPTER 4

● Before reading, begin with a discussion of ways we celebrate Christmas now in the twentieth century. Do not tell them how Laura's Christmases were spent. Tell the class to listen carefully to hear how children of long ago spent their holidays.

After reading this chapter, ask students to divide a sheet of paper in half. Label one column "Christmas"; head the other column with "Laura and Mary's Christmas." Have students list some of their own Christmas gifts, then those of Laura and Mary. When the lists are complete, create a new Venn diagram that shows presents that are still popular among children today.

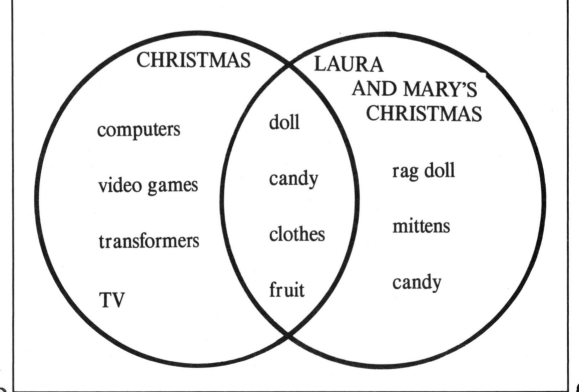

CHRISTMAS     LAURA AND MARY'S CHRISTMAS

computers     doll     rag doll

video games     candy     mittens

transformers     clothes

TV     fruit     candy

Copyright © 1989, Good Apple, Inc.

GA1052

- Discuss similarities and differences between the two lists.

- On page 60, the word *whittled* is used. As a homework assignment, ask students to locate the word in the dictionary and define it on paper. Ask them to check at home for any whittled objects which they can bring to class to share with others.

- On page 62 there are eight different foods Ma prepared for Christmas dinner: salt-rising bread, rye 'n' Injun bread, Swedish crackers, baked beans, salt pork and molasses, vinegar pies, dried-apple pies, and molasses-on-snow.

These recipes are found in *The Little House Cookbook* on the following pages:

Salt-Rising Bread . . . . . . . . . . . . . . . . . . . . . . . . . . .page 75
Swedish Crackers . . . . . . . . . . . . . . . . . . . . . . . . . .page 90
Baked Beans . . . . . . . . . . . . . . . . . . . . . . . . . . . . . .page 26
Salt Pork. . . . . . . . . . . . . . . . . . . . . . . . . . . . .pages 18-19
Vinegar Pies . . . . . . . . . . . . . . . . . . . . . . . . . . . .page 197
Dried-Apple Pies. . . . . . . . . . . . . . . . . . . . . . . . . .page 130
Molasses-on-Snow Candy . . . . . . . . . . . . . . . . . .page 192

Choose one that can be made at school as an in-class project. Ask children to bring specific ingredients from home. Have them check with their parents for instructions on how that dish is made today. Compare recipes. How are they different? How are they similar? Let students have the "finished product."

# CHAPTER 5

- Read Chapter 5 with no introduction until coming to "The Story of Grandpa's Sled and the Pig" which begins on page 87.

- Go on to read how Grandpa was a bad boy on Sunday. Read the story in its entirety without interruption.

- At the conclusion of the chapter, divide the class into groups of 4-6 students. Ask each group to discuss among themselves what *they* do on Sundays. Give each group a large sheet of white construction paper. Using a ruler, ask each group to divide the paper into 4-6 even blocks (depending on group number). Ask each student to draw a picture of what he/she does on Sunday in one of the boxes. Each student signs his/her box. When finished, each group shares with the class its pictures.

Copyright © 1989, Good Apple, Inc.

GA1052

# CHAPTER 6

- Read Chapter 6 beginning on page 101 without interruption until coming to "The Story of Pa and the Bear in the Way."

- Before beginning Pa's story, discuss Laura's adventure with the bear. Would you have been frightened? Why? What would you do if you were confronted with a bear?

- Read "The Story of Pa and the Bear in the Way" in its entirety (pages 109-114).

- Draw a picture of what Pa saw. Why do our imaginations "run away" with us? Do we convince ourselves to be scared before we have good reason to be? Discuss how we get frightened before we have reason to. Have students relate stories that have happened to them.

After finishing the story, give each child a sheet of white construction paper. Assign students the task of drawing a picture of what Pa saw. The picture is entitled "What Scared Pa?" After all drawings are complete, children share their drawings with each other and have a discussion centered upon the following questions:

a. Why do our imaginations sometimes "run away" with us?

b. Do we sometimes convince ourselves to be scared before we have good reason to be?

Allow each student the opportunity to share with the class a personal experience where he/she was frightened without reason.

Copyright © 1989, Good Apple, Inc.

GA1052

# CHAPTER 7

- Read Chapter 7 in its entirety.
- Divide the class into groups of 4 or 5 students. Each group will report on one of the following segments in the story of making maple syrup:

  a. Where is maple sugar made?
  b. How is maple sugar made?
  c. What uses are made of maple sugar?
  d. How was maple sugar made when Laura was a child?
  e. How is maple syrup made today?

Even though each group reports on only one phase of the topic, students will become involved in other aspects of the operation to answer their own responsibility. Provide students with resources they will need, either from the school or local library. Each group must also elect a "writer," to complete the final draft of the group report. All members of the group should contribute as well as provide illustrations to accompany the report. The reports can be attractively displayed on a bulletin board using the following layout.

## MAPLE SUGAR AND MAPLE SYRUP

### BULLETIN BOARD

TEACHER DIRECTIONS:

1. Yellow border
2. Use the brown tree (make branches 3-D) from page 29.
3. Cotton balls or cotton strips for snow
4. Green strips for a small amount of grass
5. Brown construction paper outlined with black marker for bucket and trough
6. Black letters for heading
7. Display group reports and illustrations

Copyright © 1989, Good Apple, Inc.

GA1052

# CHAPTER 8

- Before beginning to read Chapter 8, tell the class they will hear some words that may be unfamiliar to them. List these words on the board: *hasty pudding, corset strings,* and *jig.* Ask them to listen carefully as you read to see if they can get the meanings of these words from the context.

- Listed below are the foods that were served at Grandma's house for the dance. The page numbers indicate the locations of the recipes in *The Little House Cookbook*.

Pumpkin Pie . . . . . . . . . . . . . . . . . . . . . . . .pages 119-120
Dried Berry Pie . . . . . . . . . . . . . . . . . . . . . . .page 130
   (dried apple and raisin)
Cookies . . . . . . . . . . . . . . . . . . . . . . . . . . . .page 200
Salt-Rising Bread . . . . . . . . . . . . . . . . . . . . .pages 75-77
Pickles: Beet . . . . . . . . . . . . . . . . . . . . . . . .pages 133, 136
      Green Cucumber . . . . . . . . . . . . .pages 133, 138
      Green Tomato . . . . . . . . . . . . . .pages 133, 139

If the facilities are available, the cookie recipe can provide a fun experience for your students. Allow them to help in measuring and mixing the ingredients. Each child can spoon his or her own cookie onto the cookie sheet. After they are done, serve them as a treat while you read to them the next chapter. If facilities for cooking are unavailable to you, bake them at home and bring them to class to share with your students.

Copyright © 1989, Good Apple, Inc.

GA1052

# CHAPTER 10

- This chapter deals with Laura's jealousy over Mary.

- Read the story in its entirety.

- Upon completion, discuss what it means to be jealous of someone. Explain that everyone has had feelings of jealousy at some point in their lives, and it is a perfectly normal but less than desirable trait. Discuss how jealousy can be harmful and why.

- Ask them to remember a time they were jealous of someone and to write it down. They should answer the following questions in their explanation:

  a. Why did they feel as they did?
  b. How did they feel "inside"?
  c. What happened as a result of this jealousy?
  d. Was there any harm to anyone as a result of the jealousy?

Copyright © 1989, Good Apple, Inc.

GA1052

# LITTLE HOUSE IN THE BIG WOODS
## ALPHABETICAL ORDER

**TEACHER DIRECTIONS:**

Putting words in alphabetical order is a skill common to third through fifth graders. As an introduction to this work sheet, ask the class to recall some of the animals or foods they read about in *Little House in the Big Woods*. Write their words on the board at random as they are given to you. As a class, decide how they should be placed in alphabetical order. When this has been completed, pass out copies of the Alphabetical Order activity sheet and have students individually alphabetize each list.

ANSWER KEY:

a. 5,1,3,2,4   d. 2,3,1,5,4
b. 1,5,3,2,4   e. 3,2,4,1,5
c. 3,5,1,4,2

Copyright © 1989, Good Apple, Inc.

GA1052

# ALPHABETICAL ORDER

Words are listed in the dictionary in alphabetical order. Below are some of the words found in *Little House in the Big Woods*. Alphabetize each list by placing a 1 in the blank beside the word in that list that would appear first in the dictionary, a 2 beside the word that would appear next, etc.

Example:

_5_ wolf
_3_ muskrat
_4_ otter
_2_ fox
_1_ deer

a. ___ mink
___ bear
___ dog
___ cat
___ fish

b. ___ bacon
___ venison
___ pork
___ ham
___ spareribs

c. ___ meaty
___ tough
___ flaky
___ salty
___ lean

d. ___ carrots
___ potatoes
___ beets
___ turnips
___ squash

e. ___ onions
___ cheese
___ peppers
___ cabbage
___ pumpkins

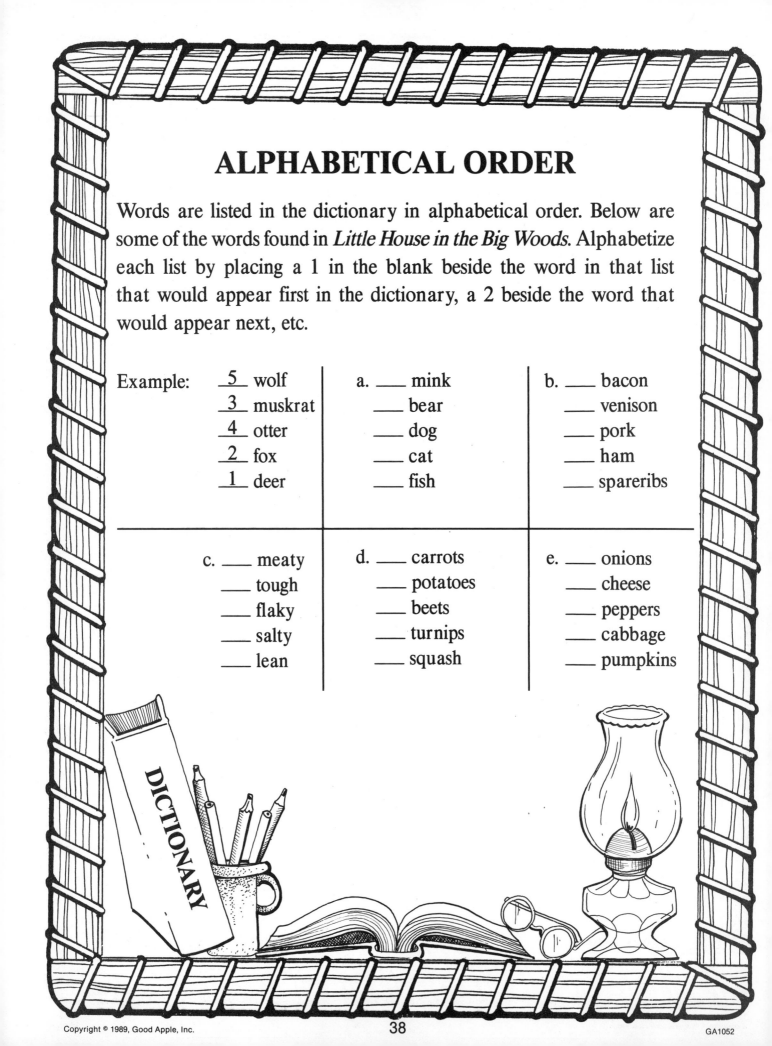

Copyright © 1989, Good Apple, Inc.

GA1052

# CLASSIFYING WORDS

**TEACHER DIRECTIONS:**

As an introduction to this work sheet, review classification of words by passing out pictures of animals, seasons or foods to several class members. Have students find other students whose pictures belong in a similar category. After all students have found a group with which they can associate, have the class (as a group) classify each group. Give each student a copy of the activity. Remind students that this time the category is given, and they must put each word under the proper heading.

ANSWER KEY:

| Animals | Meats | Days of the Week |
|---|---|---|
| panther | pork | Monday |
| mink | sausage | Tuesday |
| fox | venison | Wednesday |
| pig | smoked ham | Thursday |
| bear | | Friday |
| | | Saturday |
| | | Sunday |

Copyright © 1989, Good Apple, Inc.

GA1052

# CLASSIFYING WORDS

The words below are ones you read about in *Little House in the Big Woods*. They are mixed up and need to be classified in their correct categories. Put them where they belong by writing each word under the proper heading.

| | | | |
|---|---|---|---|
| pork | sausage | fall | Sunday |
| Monday | fox | Wednesday | Thursday |
| summer | spring | Friday | bear |
| panther | Tuesday | winter | smoked ham |
| mink | venison | pig | Saturday |

| Seasons | Animals |
|---|---|
| Example: summer<br>spring<br>winter<br>fall | |

| Days of the Week | Meats |
|---|---|
| | |

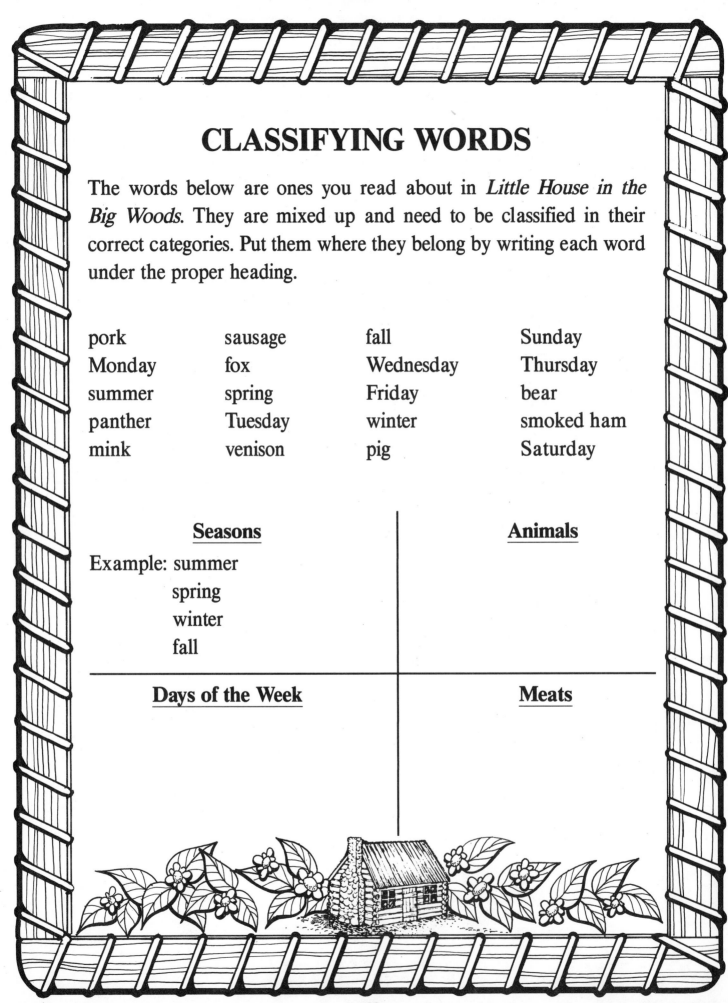

Copyright © 1989, Good Apple, Inc.
GA1052

# UNIT 2
# LITTLE HOUSE ON
# THE PRAIRIE

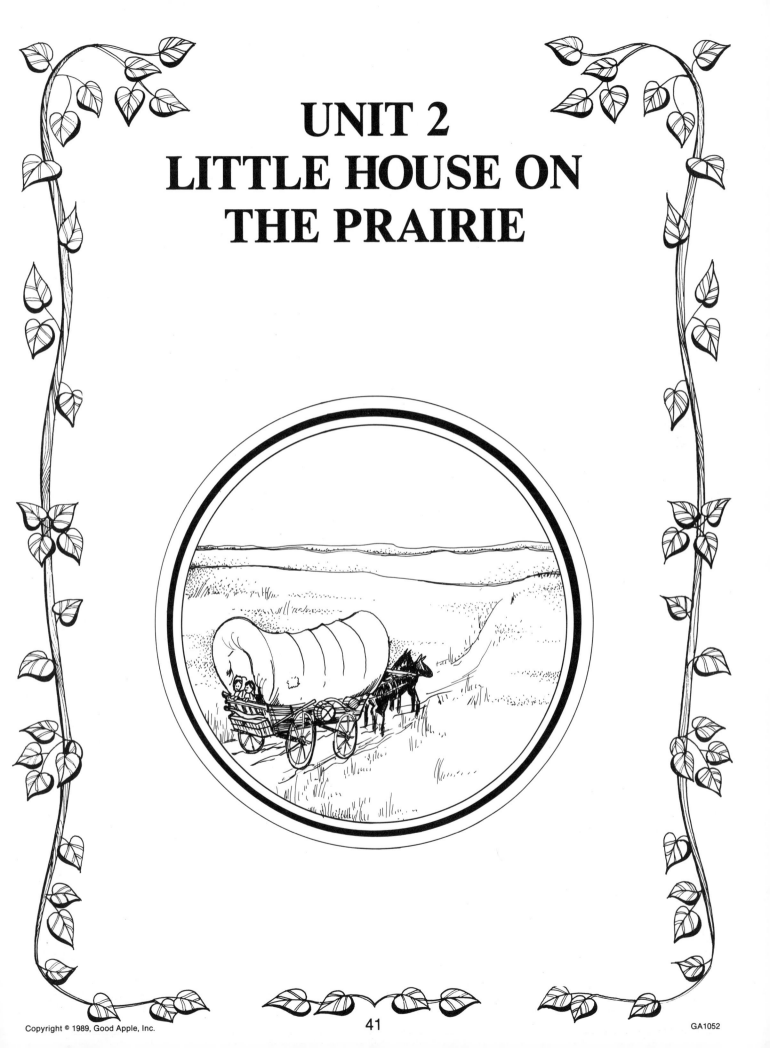

Copyright © 1989, Good Apple, Inc.

GA1052

# UNIT 2

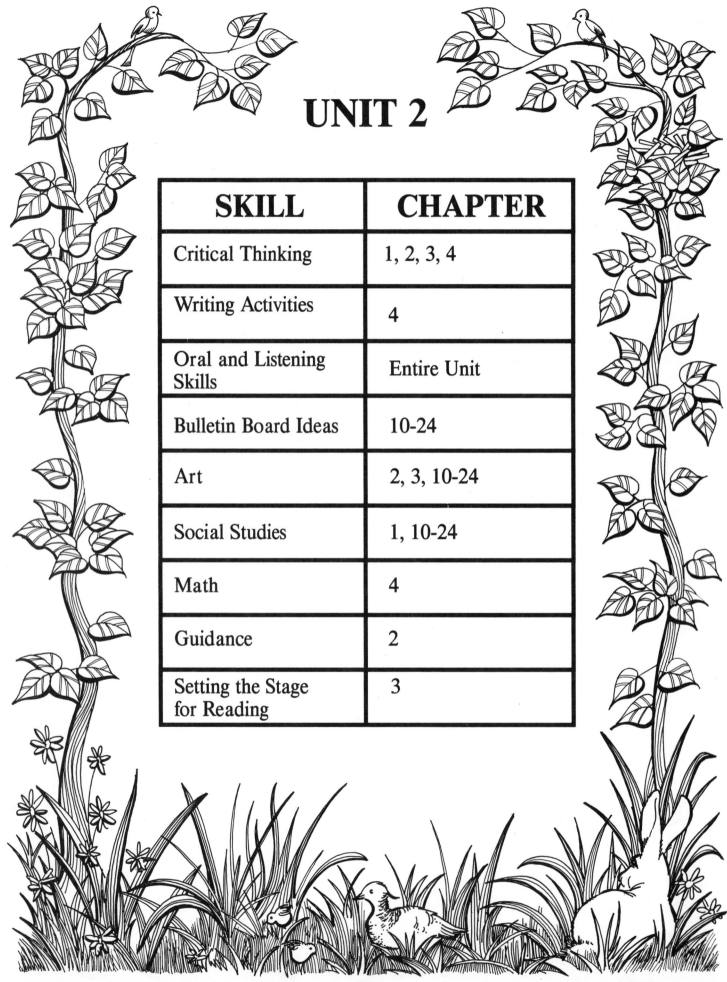

| SKILL | CHAPTER |
|---|---|
| Critical Thinking | 1, 2, 3, 4 |
| Writing Activities | 4 |
| Oral and Listening Skills | Entire Unit |
| Bulletin Board Ideas | 10-24 |
| Art | 2, 3, 10-24 |
| Social Studies | 1, 10-24 |
| Math | 4 |
| Guidance | 2 |
| Setting the Stage for Reading | 3 |

Copyright © 1989, Good Apple, Inc.

GA1052

# UNIT 2

# LITTLE HOUSE ON THE PRAIRIE

Charles Ingalls thought there were too many people in the Big Woods of Wisconsin. So Pa, Ma, Mary, Laura and Baby Carrie piled into the wagon for the long journey across the prairie toward the west.

Their journey took them into a place commonly called Indian Territory. In Indian Territory, Laura encountered many new adventures as well as hardships. This book, however, like all of the "Little House" books, shows the togetherness of the Ingalls family and what little girls did to help their families even though they were very young.

Copyright © 1989, Good Apple, Inc.                                      GA1052

# CHAPTER 1

- Show a map of Kansas. A reproducible map is found on page 45.

- Show a map of the United States. Have students compare the state of Kansas with their own state.

- The students should then locate the state of Kansas on their own copies of the United States map and color it red.

- Begin reading Chapter 1. On page 5, the words *bullet-pouch* and *powder-horn* are used. These words were introduced in Unit 1. Ask students to recall their meanings.

- The word *papoose* is used on page 6. Ask the class if anyone knows what a papoose is. Look the word up in the dictionary. If possible, bring in a picture of a papoose or an Indian doll with one. Students may bring in examples, also.

- On page 9, the state of Minnesota is mentioned. Point out the state on a United States map.

- On page 10, the Missouri River is mentioned. Point out the river on a United States map.

- Continue reading the remainder of Chapter 1 without interruption.

Copyright © 1989, Good Apple, Inc.

GA1052

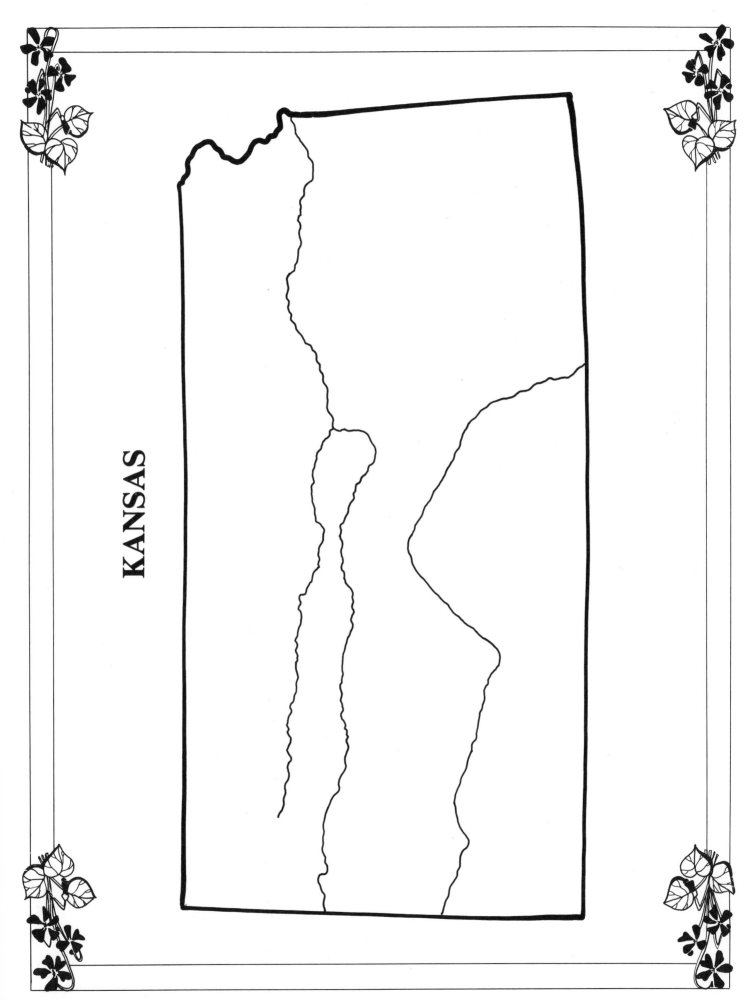

KANSAS

Copyright © 1989, Good Apple, Inc.

GA1052

# CHAPTER 2

- Ask the following review questions over Chapter 1:

  a. Why was the Ingalls family leaving the Big Woods?
  b. Where were they going?
  c. What is a bullet-pouch? A powder-horn? A papoose?
  d. What large river did the wagon cross?

- Read Chapter 2 in its entirety interspersing the following:

  a. On page 24, Laura realizes Jack did not make it across the rushing water. Ask the class how they thought Laura felt? Discuss losing something (pet, doll, stuffed animal—not humans) that was dear to you. How did you feel?

  b. On page 25, Laura says it was shameful to cry. Discuss why back in Laura's day it was shameful to cry. Is it shameful to cry in today's society? Why do people cry? Explore the emotion of sadness.

  c. Show several pictures of people who are sad. Ask the class why they think these people are sad. How do they feel when they are sad? What makes them sad?

  d. At the conclusion of the discussion, divide the class into small groups. Have each group find pictures of people who are sad and make a collage. Groups may then exchange collages and discuss the various ways sadness is shown on the faces in the collages.

Copyright © 1989, Good Apple, Inc.

GA1052

# CHAPTER 3

- Ask these review questions over Chapter 2.

    a. What were the names of the Ingalls' horses?
    b. Why did Pa jump into the rushing water?
    c. What happened to Jack?

- Introduce Chapter 3 by listing on the board some words the students will hear that may be unfamiliar to them. Does anyone know the definitions of the words?

    a. unharnessed
    b. picket-lines
    c. picket-pins
    d. coffee-mill
    e. iron bake oven
    f. iron spider

- Begin reading Chapter 3, reminding students to listen for these words, because most of them will be defined in context.

- On page 32, the Ingalls heard a long, wailing howl. What did Laura and her family hear?

- Continue reading until reaching the statement on page 33 which tells about the green eyes shining in the dark. Leave open-ended. Ask the class what scared Laura? Do not answer orally, but ask them to draw pictures of what they think these green eyes looked like.

- After ample time has passed, discuss orally what the students have drawn.

- Read the remainder of the story uninterrupted.

Copyright © 1989, Good Apple, Inc.

GA1052

# CHAPTER 4

- Ask that the following words from Chapter 3 be defined on paper as a review:

  a. iron-spider     c. picket-lines     e. unharnessed

  b. picket-pins     d. iron bake oven     f. coffee-mill

- Read this chapter in its entirety.

- This recipe can be found on the following pages of *The Little House Cookbook:*

  Pancakes.....................................pages 94-95

  As a class make pancakes for breakfast. Have students bring specific ingredients from home. Ask them to check with their parents on how pancakes are made today. Compare recipes. You may invite the principal, librarian and secretary to breakfast if the class wishes!

Copyright © 1989, Good Apple, Inc.

48

GA1052

# CHAPTER 6-24

- Beginning with Chapter 6, the usual format of activities will be changed. Chapters 6-9 can be read in their entirety without activities, though the following discussions can take place if so desired.

CHAPTER 6: Discuss moving from one place to another. Is this difficult?

CHAPTER 7: Wolves! What do they look like? Where do they live? Have you ever seen one?

CHAPTER 8: Discuss making your home all by yourself. What would you need? Is this the way your house was built? Is your door built with hinges and a latchstring? What is a latchstring?

CHAPTER 9: What is a hearth? Does your house have one? It is said that in some cultures the hearth is the most important place in the house. Why? What do you do around the hearth in your home?

- Beginning with Chapter 10, the Ingalls begin to encounter the Indians. This is an excellent opportunity to study the Indian tribe called the Osage which the Ingalls met in Indian Territory. This opportunity leads to the study of all North American Indians. The following is a suggested plan of study.

# CHAPTERS 6-24 (cont'd.)

1. Read Chapter 11 in its entirety. At its conclusion, tell the children that they will be studying American Indians while the remainder of the book is being read. Tell them there will be activities done as well as one required report.

2. Begin your discussion of American Indians by talking about this place called Indian Territory. According to our book, *Little House on the Prairie*, Pa and his family lived in Kansas, though the book later states they built their little house in Oklahoma. According to Donald Zochert, author of *Laura, the Life of Laura Ingalls Wilder*, the Ingalls were indeed in Kansas. Maps of Indian Territory, however, show its location in Oklahoma (a reproducible map can be found on page 51). The Osage Indians, however, were in *both* Kansas and Oklahoma. Perhaps Ma and Pa simply called this place Indian Territory (if they did indeed live in Kansas) since Indians were on the land first.

3. Place on the chalkboard a listing of the Indian tribes below.

| | | | | |
|---|---|---|---|---|
| Algonquin | Creek | Maidu | Navaho | Sauk |
| Apache* | Croaton | Makah | Nez Perce´ | Seminole |
| Arapaho* | Crow | Malecite | Nootka | Shawnee* |
| Arikara | Delaware* | Mandan | Ojibwa | Shoshoni* |
| Bannock | Erie* | Massachusetts | Omaha | Sioux* |
| Blackfoot* | Flathead | Menominee* | Osage* | Tarascan* |
| Caddo | Haida | Miami* | Ottawa | Tlingit* |
| Cherokee* | Hidata* | Micmac | Paiute* | Tsimshian |
| Cheyenne* | Hopi* | Modoc | Pawnee | Ute |
| Chickasaw | Hupa | Mohave | Pequot | Wichita |
| Chinook | Huron | Mohegan* | Pima | Winnebago |
| Choctaw | Kiowa | Narraganset | Pomo | Yakima |
| Comanche* | Klamath | Naskapi | Potawatomi | Yamasee |
| Conestoga | Kutenai | Natchez* | Powhatan | Zuni |
| Cree | Kwakuitl | | | |

(*may be most familiar)

4. Tell the students they will be responsible for doing a report on one of the listed tribes. Encyclopedias are to be used and students will be given time to use the school library. The reports are to be one page long and should contain as much information as they can find about the tribes chosen. The reports are due when Chapter 24 is completed (approximately two weeks because of other activities on Indians).

Copyright © 1989, Good Apple, Inc.
GA1052

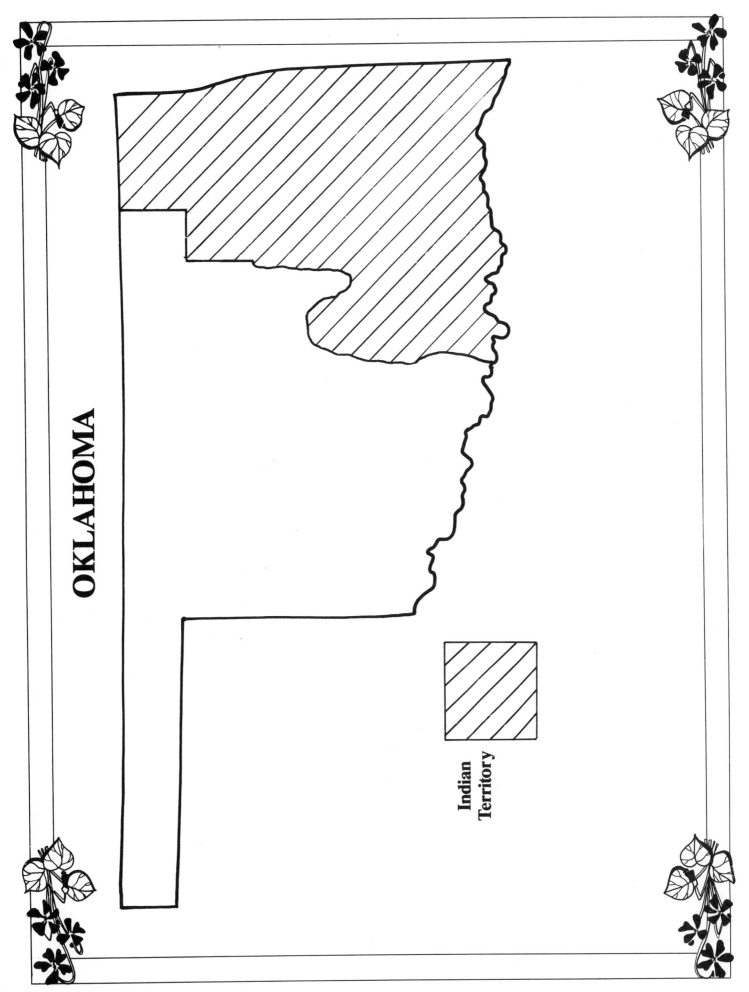

OKLAHOMA

Indian
Territory

Copyright © 1989, Good Apple, Inc.

51

GA1052

The following four art activities may be interspersed throughout Chapters 10-24 and may be used for bulletin boards.

## INDIAN HEADDRESS

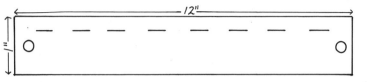

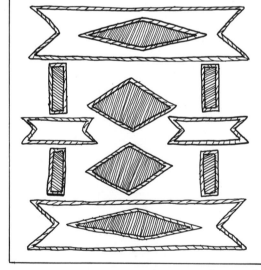

**SUPPLIES:**
1″ x 12″ (2.56 cm x 30.72 cm)
    piece of black construction
    paper
string
scissors
colored construction paper
    strips for feathers or real
    feathers from a hobby
    shop

**STUDENT DIRECTIONS:**
Cut small horizontal slits (½″ [1.28 cm] wide) along black strip. Punch one hole in each end of strip. Tie string (one piece) at each end of strip. Place colored feathers in slits. If making feathers, follow pattern above.

## YARN RUGS

**SUPPLIES:**
1 large piece of tagboard
various colors of yarn
pencil
glue
crayon

**STUDENT DIRECTIONS:**
With pencil, draw design of an Indian rug on tagboard. After drawing, run glue along each line and place colorful yarn on the line. In between yarn, color with crayons.

Copyright © 1989, Good Apple, Inc.

GA1052

# INDIAN BEADS

**SUPPLIES:**
   small butter dish
   colored macaroni
      (various shapes)
   string

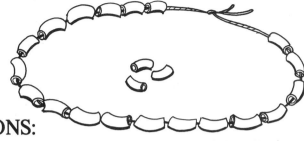

**STUDENT DIRECTIONS:**
   Place various colored macaroni in butter dish. String different shaped macaroni on string. (Place a book on one end of string so macaroni will not slip off.) Knot ends of string, leaving enough to tie around neck.

**TEACHER DIRECTIONS:**
   Use elbow macaroni, small stovepipe, sewer pipe, etc. To color macaroni, place in a large plastic bag; shake in several drops of food coloring; close bag tightly and shake. Use these colors: black, red, blue, and yellow.

# CHALK HEADS

**SUPPLIES:**
   9″ x 12″ (23.04 cm x 30.72 cm)
      piece of black construction
      paper
   colored chalk

**TEACHER AND STUDENT DIRECTIONS:**
   Find a picture of an Indian in a book or encyclopedia. Draw the head of the Indian with chalk only. Blend in color with Kleenex (demonstrate this technique).

At the conclusion of reading *Little House on the Prairie*, the work sheet on the following page can be used as a culminating activity.

Copyright © 1989, Good Apple, Inc.

GA1052

# SCRAMBLED TRIBES

Place the scrambled letters in correct order to form the names of North American tribes.

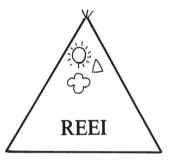

_____   _____   _____

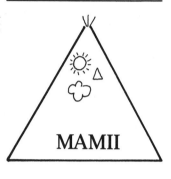

_____   _____   _____

_____   _____   _____

_____   _____   _____

Copyright © 1989, Good Apple, Inc.

GA1052

# UNIT 3
# ON THE BANKS OF
# PLUM CREEK

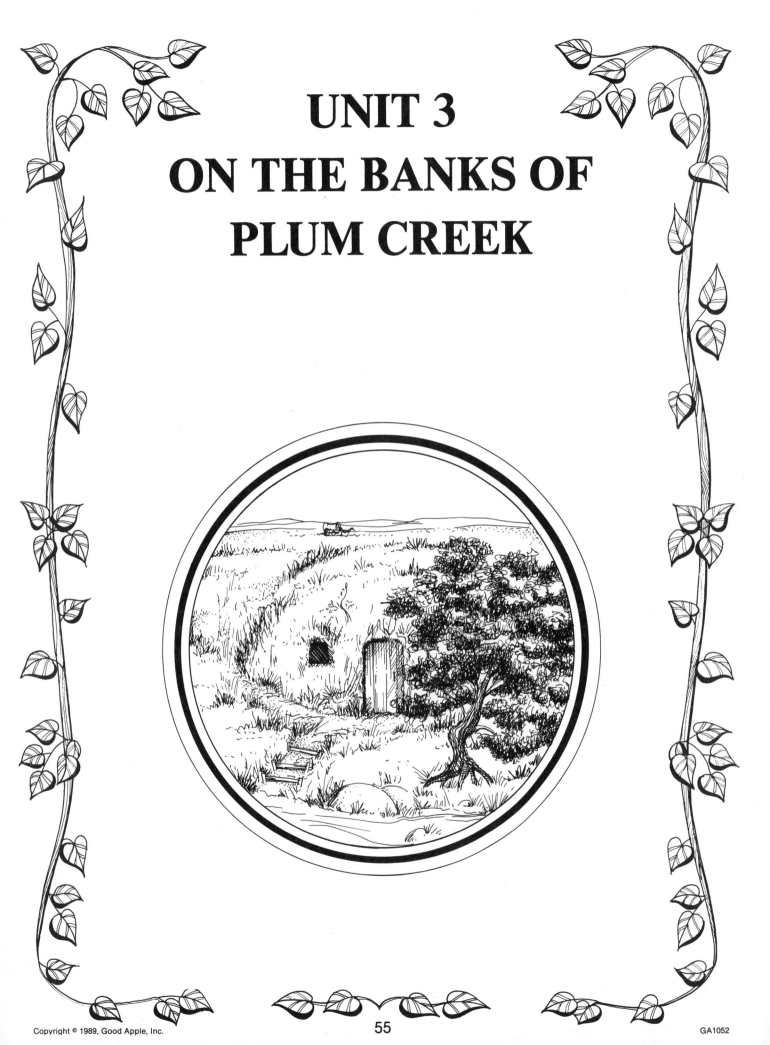

Copyright © 1989, Good Apple, Inc.

GA1052

# UNIT 3

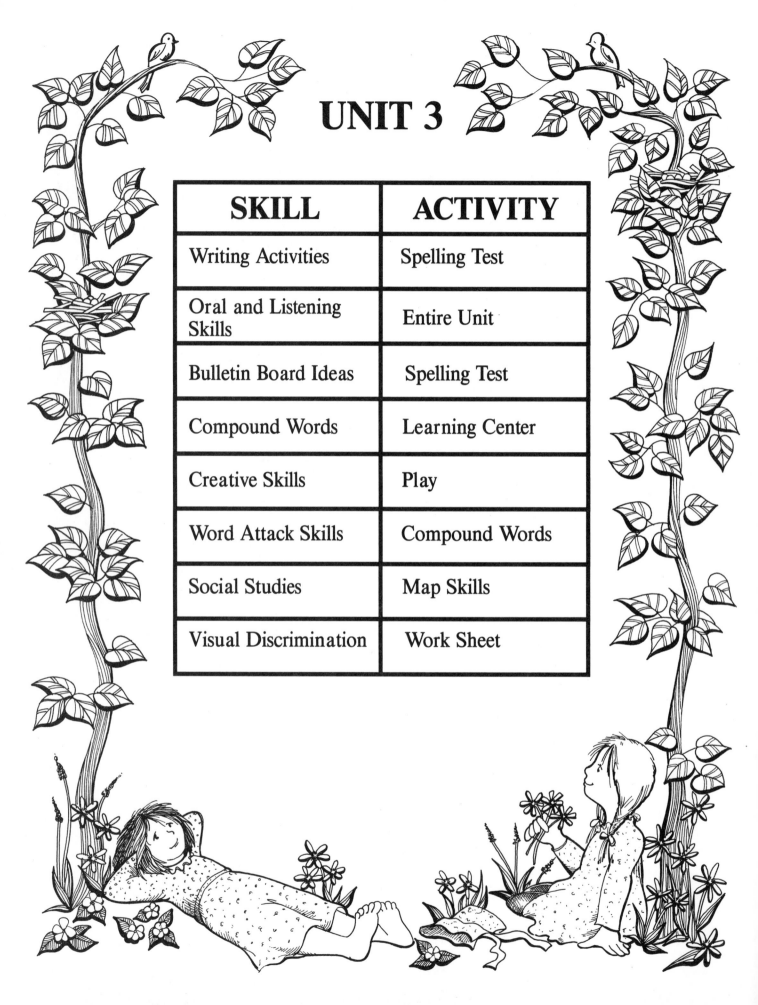

| SKILL | ACTIVITY |
|---|---|
| Writing Activities | Spelling Test |
| Oral and Listening Skills | Entire Unit |
| Bulletin Board Ideas | Spelling Test |
| Compound Words | Learning Center |
| Creative Skills | Play |
| Word Attack Skills | Compound Words |
| Social Studies | Map Skills |
| Visual Discrimination | Work Sheet |

Copyright © 1989, Good Apple, Inc.

GA1052

# UNIT 3
# ON THE BANKS OF PLUM CREEK

Plum Creek was the third home for the Ingalls family. Only this time the house was underground and called a dugout.

There are many new adventures and discoveries in this book. The theme remains consistent as in the two previous books, but it is in this one that the mischievous Laura appears. Laura has her first run-in with Nellie Oleson and soon learns how to "get back" at the very jealous Nellie!

Children can relate to this particular Laura Ingalls Wilder book because of Laura's school experiences. Neither Laura nor Mary had ever gone to school and actually were not pleased with the prospect. Upon arriving their first day, they were greeted with laughter from the other children because their skirts were too short compared to the "town girls." Most students will find their hearts going out to the Ingalls girls who must learn to "fit in."

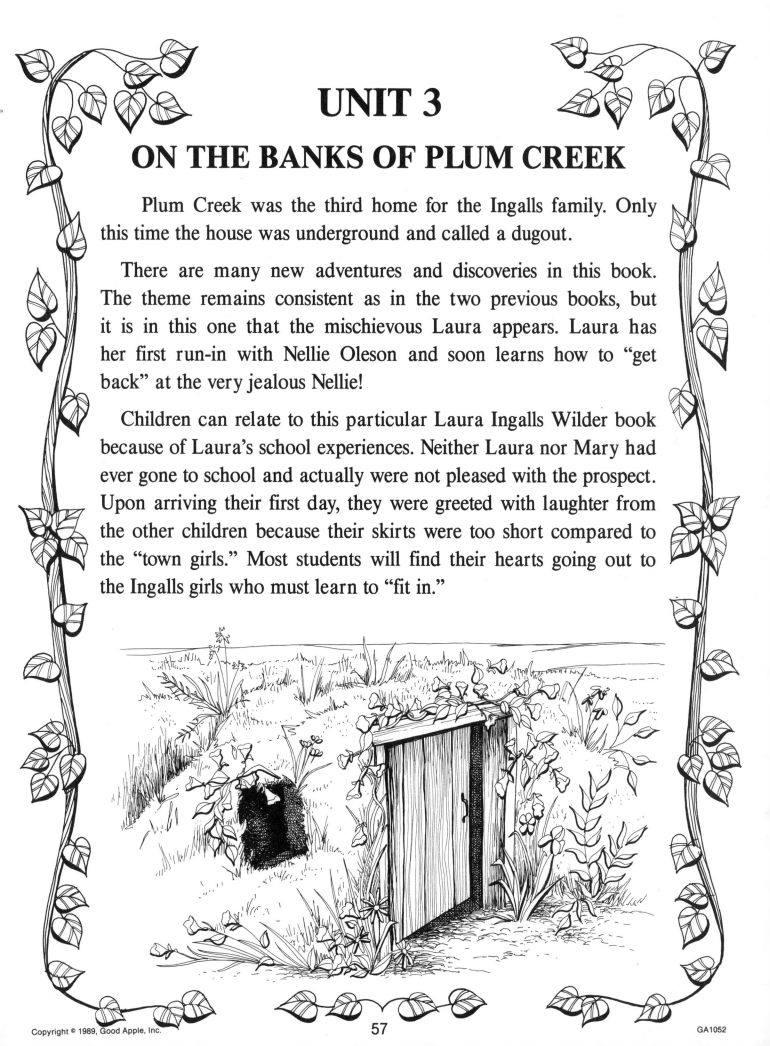

Copyright © 1989, Good Apple, Inc.

GA1052

# STORY INTRODUCTION

When the time comes to read *On the Banks of Plum Creek*, you will find that the children have become well-acquainted with the Ingalls family. Therefore, a diversion from previously explored activities can occur.

- Show a map of Minnesota. Locate Walnut Grove. A reproducible map is found on page 59.

- Show a map of the United States. Have students compare the state of Minnesota with their own state.

- The students should then locate the state of Minnesota on their own copies of the United States map and color it green.

- Read *On the Banks of Plum Creek* to the students in its entirety while interspersing the following activities.

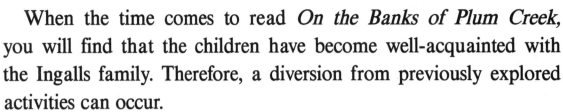

# COMPOUND WORDS

## LEARNING CENTER

Laminate the words on pages 60 and 61 and cut out. Place BOX A words in one box and BOX B words in another. Put both boxes at a learning center and instruct students to complete the compound words by matching one word from each box. Provide children with an answer key.

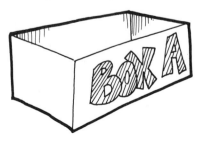
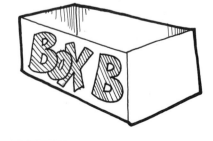

Copyright © 1989, Good Apple, Inc.

GA1052

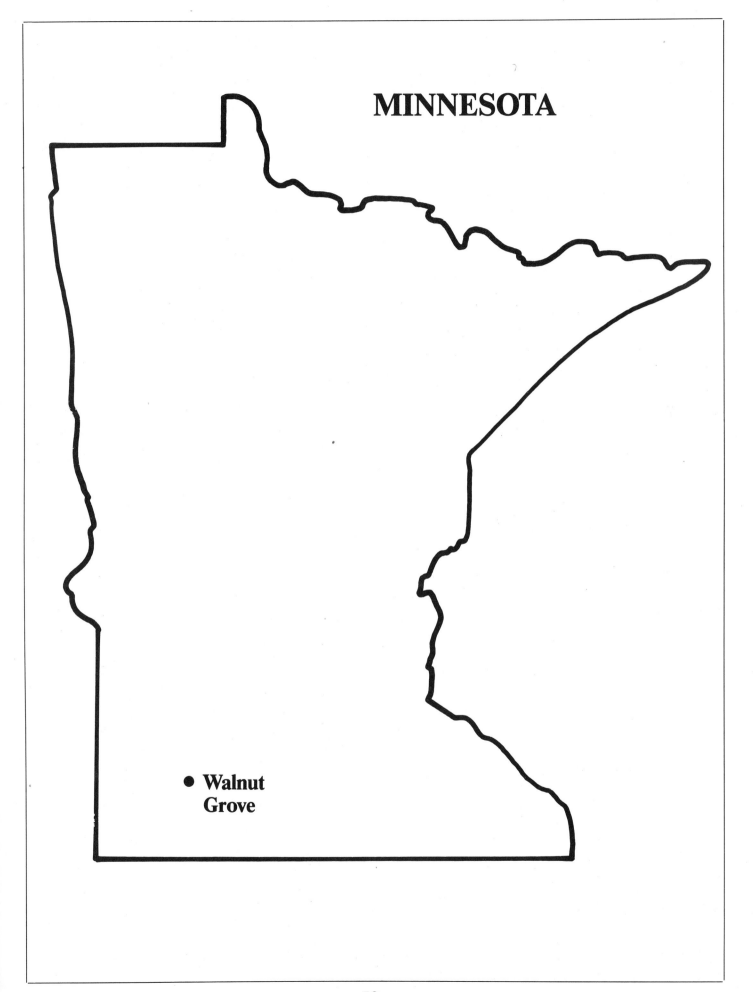

# MINNESOTA

● **Walnut Grove**

Copyright © 1989, Good Apple, Inc.

59

GA1052

| | |
|---|---|
| bed | after |
| day | sun |
| over | grass |
| foot | any |
| butter | straw |

Copyright © 1989, Good Apple, Inc.

GA1052

# BOX B

| | |
|---|---|
| room | noon |
| time | shine |
| time | hopper |
| prints | thing |
| flies | stack |

Copyright © 1989, Good Apple, Inc.

GA1052

# PLUM CREEK
# SUPER SPELLERS!
### BULLETIN BOARD

School is a primary focus of this particular Wilder book, and this suggestion for a bulletin board keeps this in mind. On the following page is a reproducible which can be used for weekly spelling tests. Encourage students to put extra effort into studying their weekly word lists, since perfect papers will be displayed on the Plum Creek Super Spellers bulletin board!

## TEACHER DIRECTIONS:
1. Green border
2. Yellow letters for heading
3. Green and yellow construction paper to mount reproducibles
4. One reproducible per student

Copyright © 1989, Good Apple, Inc.

GA1052

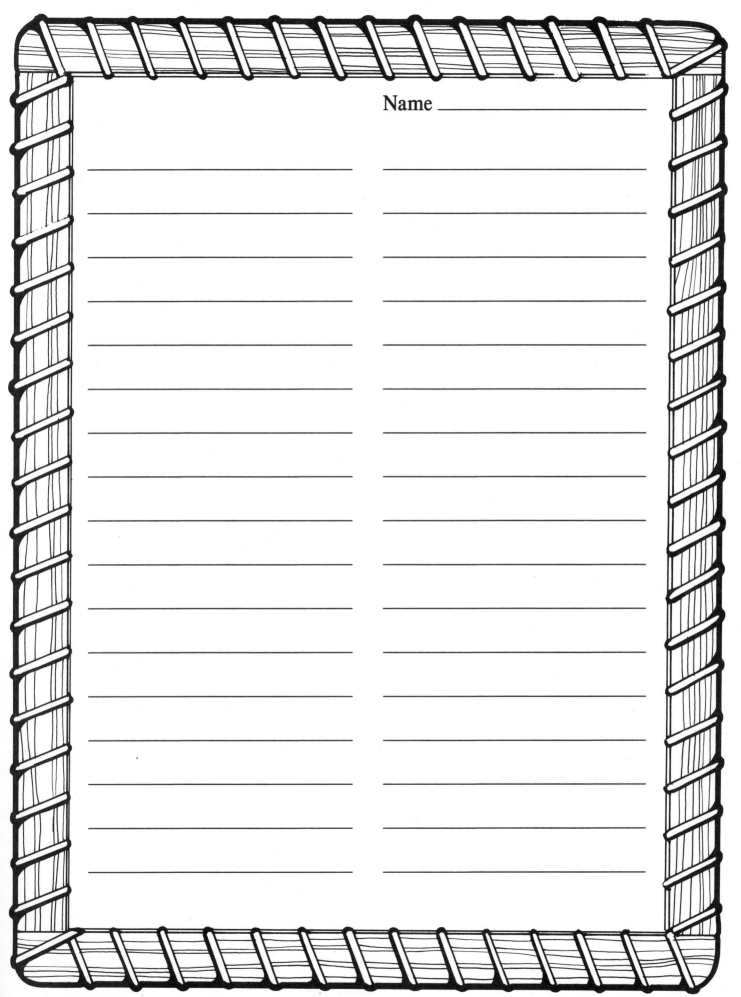

Name _____

Copyright © 1989, Good Apple, Inc.

63

GA1052

# WORD SEARCH PUZZLE

## TEACHER DIRECTIONS:

Most children are familiar with this type of puzzle, but instead of simply passing it out for individual completion, try the following:

1. Make an overhead of the puzzle and do the puzzle as a group.
2. Divide the class into groups of three to four students and see which group can complete the puzzle first. As a reward, each group member may read a page from *On the Banks of Plum Creek* orally.
3. Pass out a puzzle to each student. Start the clock. The first child finished gets a paperback copy of *On the Banks of Plum Creek*!

## ANSWER KEY:

```
X A C B J Q Z C D F G H B A B C D E E
Y J K B L M N X A V W X Y Z I A B I C
D B C L I J D K L M R X W P B S L R P
A Q R O A F I H G I L A M R L L C I E
C S I O E B V N V O S T I G E K J A E
E V T D J K A W U G B D F N U V W C H
G C A S T U D Y K R R P Q Y D Y Z J K
H B H U A D Z C L A S T X C D R I X B
B A R C M N O X O S N M L Y M L O J K
K I F K F P W P S S H I Z A F A M P O
M J D E G V U D I H B C D G B L N P S
S K B R E V T U G O E D C R Q R F Z A
O U A S C A R E D P R D R A Z Z I L B
Q U R V H B H W F P E O R S Z A I L B
S X T P U C S X Y E C W X S Y Z P Q R
U B A Z R A R Z J R F G H H O I J T S
W X Y Z C I A W D S D I N O U Z V W X
Y V Q S H N S B C E P B N P A G H A B
Z C B R M O S E J L O X Y P C H L N P
A S P I Q U T K P M W D Z E C J K L S
C V Q J R P Q R T V U E F R I K M O A
E X R A Q S V N O C H R I S T M A S M
```

Copyright © 1989, Good Apple, Inc.

GA1052

# WORD SEARCH PUZZLE

Can you find these words hidden in the puzzle? Look up, down, diagonally, forward or backward!

| | | |
|---|---|---|
| crab | Nellie | surprise |
| raindrops | Sam | grasshoppers |
| scared | David | blizzard |
| bloodsuckers | church | Christmas |
| study | | Bible |

```
X A C B J Q Z C D F G H B A B C D E E
Y J K B L M N X A V W X Y Z I A B I C
D B C L I J D K L M R X W P B S L R P
A Q R O A F I H G I L A M R L L C I E
C S I O E B V N V O S T I G E K J A E
E V T D J K A W U G B D F N U V W C H
G C A S T U D Y K R R P Q Y D Y Z J K
H B H U A D Z C L A S T X C D R I X B
B A R C M N O X O S N M L Y M L O J K
K I F K F P W P S S H I Z A F A M P O
M J D E G V U D I H B C D G B L N P S
S K B R E V T U G O E D C R Q R F Z A
O U A S C A R E D P R D R A Z Z I L B
Q U R V H B H W F P E O R S Z A I L B
S X T P U C S X Y E C W X S Y Z P Q R
U B A Z R A R Z J R F G H H O I J T S
W X Y Z C I A W D S D I N O U Z V W X
Y V Q S H N S B C E P B N P A G H A B
Z C B R M O S E J L O X Y P C H L N P
A S P I Q U T K P M W D Z E C J K L S
C V Q J R P Q R T V U E F R I K M O A
E X R A Q S V N O C H R I S T M A S M
```

Copyright © 1989, Good Apple, Inc.

GA1052

# CULMINATING ACTIVITY

## PLAY

Chapters used for this play are loosely based on Chapters 2, 20, 21 and 41. Props for the play should be kept to classroom equipment—chairs, desks, books, shelves, tables, etc. Students portraying characters should, with their parents help, create simple costumes at home.

This play can be put on in one of two ways:

1. With the principal's help, allow students to put on the play at a school assembly. The assembly need be only thirty minutes in length. Choose one student not in the play to write and give the audience background information on Laura and her family as well as a short introduction to the play.

2. The children can put on a Laura Ingalls Wilder Night as part of the school's monthly PTA/PTO meeting. As above, one student should write and introduce the play to the audience. At the conclusion, students can serve punch and cookies!

Copyright © 1989, Good Apple, Inc.

GA1052

# ON THE BANKS OF PLUM CREEK

## A PLAY

CHARACTERS:    Pa  
                       Ma  
                       Mary  
                       Laura  
                       Teacher  
                       Narrator  
                       Nellie Oleson  
                       Christy Kennedy  
                       Other children to portray students

## SCENE I

Ma, Mary, and Laura are busy fixing up their new home—a dugout. Baby Carrie is asleep. Pa is working in the fields.

NARRATOR: Pa, Ma, Mary, Laura and Baby Carrie had been told to leave Indian Territory by the government just as all the other settlers had. So, again, the wagon was packed. Their destination was Minnesota where Pa would trade for their new little house—a dugout—which is a place dug out from the side of a hill.

MA: Well, girls, your Pa was right, this dugout *is* clean. I believe with a little time we can make it look just like home. Mary, Laura, please fill the water pails.

(Mary and Laura go off stage to get the water pails. Mary carries a larger one than Laura.)

MARY: Here, Ma. Laura will go get the water in the creek. (Laura exits.)

(Ma and Mary are busy sweeping the dugout.)

LAURA: Here, Ma; here's the water. Ma, can I go play at the footbridge? I'll—

MA: May, Laura.

LAURA: May I go play at the footbridge? I'll be careful—please.

MA: No, Laura. Your Pa will be in soon, and we have to get what we can from the wagon.

LAURA: OK, Ma. (sadly)

(Pa enters.)

PA: Well, Caroline, what do you think?

MA: It's nice, Charles, and you were right, the place is very clean and pleasant. But, Charles, what about the beds? There is no real floor.

| | |
|---|---|
| **PA:** | No problem, Caroline. I'll spread willow boughs down to put the beds on until I can make some bedsteads. (Pa begins to leave.) |
| **LAURA:** | (running to him) Can I help, Pa, please? |
| **PA:** | Well, OK, Half-Pint, come on along. |
| | (Pa and Laura leave hand in hand.) |
| | (Mary and Ma continue to clean and arrange while Pa and Laura collect willow boughs.) |
| **PA:** | Here you are, Caroline. (Pa is placing boughs on floor.) Now, we can turn in for the night. |
| | (Lights fade out.) |

## SCENE II

Inside the dugout, Ma is getting Mary and Laura ready for school. Pa is seated at the table and Carrie is playing nearby.

| | |
|---|---|
| **NARRATOR:** | The dugout turned out to be a wonderful place to live! Laura loved to play on the footbridge and in the creek. The creek had an old crab that lived there that Laura enjoyed teasing! There were also haystacks which Mary and Laura were not supposed to slide down—but they did! The Ingalls even celebrated Christmas in the dugout and the weather was very strange—it was called grasshopper weather. When the weather grew warmer in the spring, Mary and Laura were about to begin a new adventure—one they were not sure they wanted to participate in! |
| | (Ma is combing Laura's hair as Mary is properly seated at the table all dressed up.) |
| **LAURA:** | Why do we have to go to school, Pa? |
| **MA:** | Now Laura, you know your Pa and I have always wanted our girls to get a good education. You have to go, Laura; you'll like it there. You'll make lots of new friends. |
| **LAURA:** | (sadly, face down) OK, Ma. |
| | (Laura and Mary exit after Ma hands them their books.) |
| **MA:** | Be good girls. |
| **MARY:** | We will, Ma. |
| | (Mary and Laura walk slowly to school.) |
| **MARY:** | Are you scared, Laura? |
| **LAURA:** | Yes, Mary, I—. What's that noise? |
| | (The school children are loudly playing outside the schoolhouse.) |

Copyright © 1989, Good Apple, Inc.

GA1052

| | |
|---|---|
| MARY: | That must be the school. Pa said we'd hear the other children when we came close. |
| | (Mary and Laura look at each other and walk slowly on.) |
| | (As Mary and Laura approach the schoolyard, all the children stop and stare.) |
| LAURA: | What are all of you staring at? (Laura realizes what she's said and clasps her hand over her mouth.) |
| MARY: | (horrified) Laura! |
| BOYS: | (in unison and laughing) Their dresses are short; they look like snipes! (ha, ha, etc.) |
| | (Mary and Laura start to walk backwards, ready to run.) |
| | (Just then a little girl approaches.) |
| CHRISTY: | Hello, my name is Christy Kennedy. Don't mind them; they don't mean any harm. |
| | (Christy introduces Laura and Mary to all the other students.) |
| | (The teacher rings the bell, and the pupils file into the room.) |
| TEACHER: | I see we have some new students. |
| MARY: | Yes, ma'am. I'm Mary Ingalls; this is my sister Laura. |
| TEACHER: | (smiling) That's just fine. I'll put your names into my book; now let's hear you read. |
| | (Mary reads a small passage from a McGuffy reader and the teacher seats her. Laura cannot read and only shakes her head. The teacher seats her with Mary and they quietly begin to study, Mary reading in the back, Laura in the front, with the pages standing up between them.) |
| | (The teacher dismisses the class for recess.) |
| NELLIE: | Come, girls, let's play ring around the rosy. |
| | (All the girls play, but soon grow tired. The boys are busy playing elsewhere.) |
| LAURA: | I know; let's play Uncle John. |
| ALL GIRLS: | Yes, yes! (Girls gather around Laura.) |
| NELLIE: | (stomping her feet and grabbing Laura's braids) No, no, no! I don't like that game. No! |
| LAURA: | (She turns quickly and raises her hand to slap Nellie, but she stops just in time.) |
| CHRISTY: | Come, Laura. |
| | (All the girls play Uncle John.) |
| | (Light fades.) |

Copyright © 1989, Good Apple, Inc.

GA1052

## SCENE III

Dinner table in the Ingalls' home.

PA:     Well, girls, how was your first day at school?

MARY:    Oh, fine, Pa. I can read in the back of the reader.

PA:     That's fine, Mary. Laura, did you like school?

LAURA:   Yes, Pa.

MA:     Laura, did something go wrong at school?

LAURA:   No, Ma, not really. Well, there's this awful girl named Nellie who thinks she's better than Mary and me. She—.

MA:     Mary and I, Laura.

LAURA:   Yes, Ma. She's from New York and is pretty and wears nice clothes. She pulled my braids. I almost slapped her. (Laura lowers her head.)

PA:     (sternly) Laura, you must never strike anyone.

LAURA:   (head lowered) Yes, Pa.

       (Light fades.)

## SCENE IV

Interior of the Ingalls' home. Ma is just getting up; Pa is coming in from doing chores and the girls are playing.

NARRATOR:  Soon Laura and Mary liked going to school. They even attended their first party given by Nellie Oleson and in return had their own country party. Pa's wheat field was so very good, it would bring in so much money, but grasshoppers came in a glittering cloud and destroyed the crop. Pa had to go away to the east to find work, but he was soon home, and it was Christmas Eve.

PA:     The wind is rising. Looks like another blizzard.

MA:     Let it storm, Charles, just so long as we're all snug and safe.

PA:     That we are, Caroline, that we are.

LAURA:   Pa, will you play the fiddle?

PA:     Why yes, Laura, if you'll bring it to me.

       (Laura goes and gets the fiddle.)

       (Pa begins to play. All begin to sing "Jingle Bells.")

PA:     Now that was fine, just fine. Makes a man hungry after such a rousing song!

MA:     Come, Charles, girls, supper is ready.

       (All gather round the table and bow heads as Pa says grace.)

       (Light fades.)

## THE END

Copyright © 1989, Good Apple, Inc.

GA1052

# UNIT 4
# BY THE SHORES OF
# SILVER LAKE

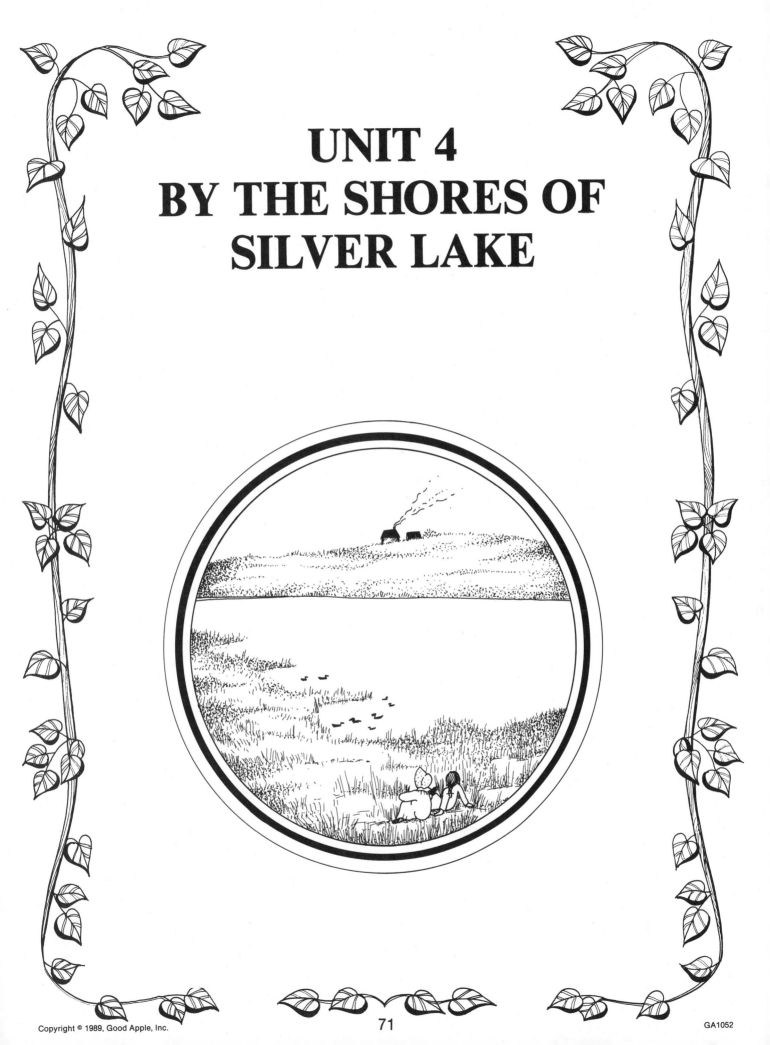

Copyright © 1989, Good Apple, Inc.

GA1052

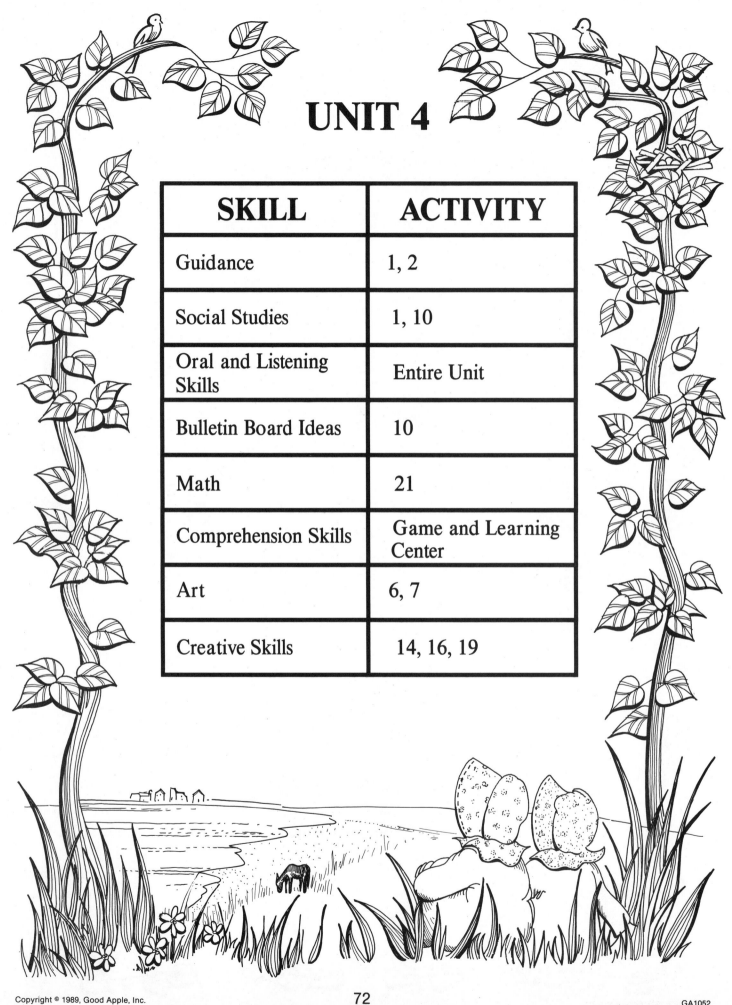

# UNIT 4

| SKILL | ACTIVITY |
| --- | --- |
| Guidance | 1, 2 |
| Social Studies | 1, 10 |
| Oral and Listening Skills | Entire Unit |
| Bulletin Board Ideas | 10 |
| Math | 21 |
| Comprehension Skills | Game and Learning Center |
| Art | 6, 7 |
| Creative Skills | 14, 16, 19 |

Copyright © 1989, Good Apple, Inc.

GA1052

# UNIT 4

## BY THE SHORES OF SILVER LAKE

Things had not gone well for the Ingalls family the two years they lived at Plum Creek, so Pa said it was time to move. They moved to De Smet in Dakota Territory and became one of the first families to settle there. They were going to make a new life for themselves at a place called Silver Lake.

Silver Lake brought many more new experiences for Laura. She took her first train ride, rode her first horse and for the first time lived in a town with other people. But Laura also had a new responsibility now that she was growing up. Mary was blind and Pa had told Laura she must now be Mary's "eyes." Laura soon realized that as we grow older there are things we must accept, even though we don't like them.

Living in town was also a hard lesson for Laura. Towns had people, and people scared her. But she overcame her fear with the help of her loving, concerned family and friends.

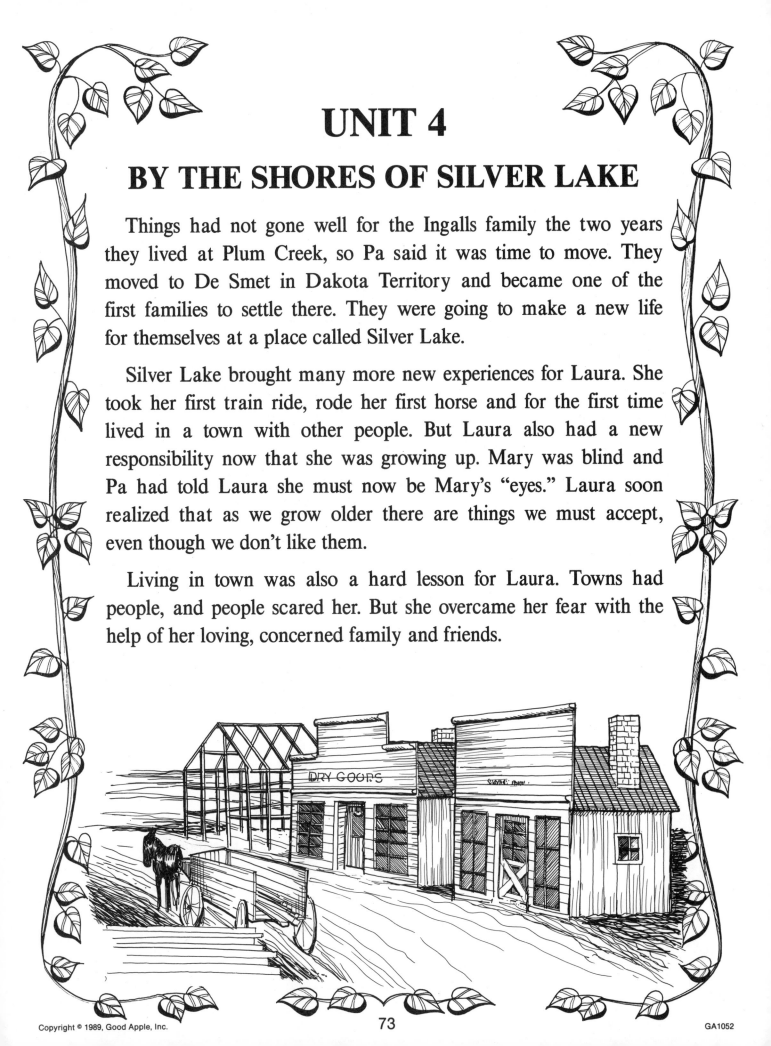

Copyright © 1989, Good Apple, Inc.

GA1052

# CHAPTER 1

- Show a map of South Dakota. Locate De Smet. A reproducible map is found on page 75.

- Show a map of the United States. Have students compare the state of South Dakota with their own state.

- The students should then locate the state of South Dakota on their own copies of the United States map and color it purple.

- Point out to the children that South Dakota is the last state the Ingalls family lived in. The remainder of the books read will take place in De Smet, South Dakota.

- Read Chapter 1 to the children in its entirety.

- The last page of the chapter (page 7) explains some of the hazards of train travel. Have students discuss some of the fears and hazards of air travel today. Compare these with the hazards of train travel during the Ingalls' day.

# CHAPTER 2

- Read Chapter 2 without interruption.

- Introduce a discussion period by asking students whether they have had a pet that has died.

- Ask how they felt. Sad? Alone? Afraid? Angry?

- Pursue their feelings by having students relate to their classmates the incidents of their pets' death.

- Read the book, *The Accident* by Carol Carrick, which deals with a boy's feelings when his dog is killed.

- Discuss the children's reactions to the book.

Copyright © 1989, Good Apple, Inc.

GA1052

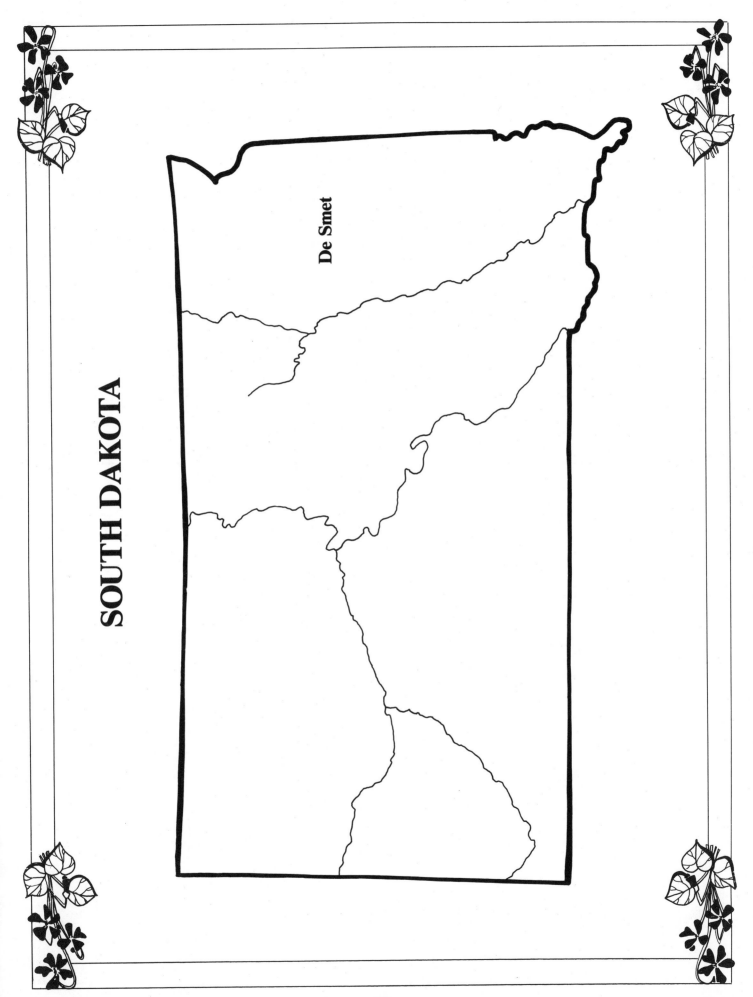

SOUTH DAKOTA

De Smet

Copyright © 1989, Good Apple, Inc.

75

GA1052

# CHAPTER 6

- This chapter gives an account of two young girls enjoying a day of fun on the prairie, a day Laura hadn't been able to enjoy since Pa had gone West several months before. Read this chapter to the class in its entirety, but read it in a carefree voice with lots of enthusiasm, a voice which will relay to your class the freedom and fun Laura and Lena were having.

- At the chapter's conclusion, ask the class to describe in a written paragraph or through a drawing how Laura and Lena looked when riding across the wide open prairie. Then have an oral discussion of how the two girls felt. Students may volunteer to either read their paragraphs or show their drawings to the class.

# CHAPTER 7

- Introduce this chapter with pictures of the prairie put up on the board.

- Read Chapter 7 in its entirety.

- On page 64, Big Jerry is mentioned for the first time. Ask the class:

  a. What do you think Big Jerry looks like?
  b. Why was Ma afraid of Big Jerry?
  c. What is a gambler? A horse thief?

- Draw a picture of Big Jerry and his snow-white horse.

- Discuss with the class how easy it was for a man to be robbed or killed in the West because there were no laws. Why is it better to have laws rather than none at all?

Copyright © 1989, Good Apple, Inc.

GA1052

# CHAPTER 10

## BULLETIN BOARD

- Beginning on page 97 of Chapter 10, Pa and Laura are watching workers build the railroad. There has been quite a change in our railroad system from the past to the present day. This chapter is an opportunity for students to study the railroad system from past to present. Ask the class to research our railroad system and do a short handwritten report on the subject. They may use any resources on hand, including those provided by you. Set no limits to what is to be said in the report except that reports should be only one sheet of notebook paper.

- The reports may be placed on the following bulletin board.

## TEACHER DIRECTIONS:
1. Black border
2. Black letters cut to read *Our Railroad, Past and Present*
3. Brown railroad tracks
4. Red and black steam engine
5. Cotton for smoke

**Our Railroad, Past and Present**

Copyright © 1989, Good Apple, Inc.

GA1052

# CHAPTER 14

- The surveyor's house! My what a huge house—with two floors, and a pantry. Why would anyone need so much space to live in? This is what Laura thought as she peered into the newest place for the Ingalls family to live. As you are reading this chapter to the class, let them know that in reality the surveyor's house was quite small, not even as big as your classroom!

- As this chapter is being read, discuss why Laura thought this house was so large.

- Conclude Chapter 14 with the following activity.

## USING DESCRIPTIVE WORDS

1. Divide the class into groups of six.

2. Give each group one of the following words on a card:

    a. surveyor    d. upstairs
    b. house       e. stove
    c. pantry      f. prairie

3. Ask students to list on a piece of notebook paper at least six descriptive words or phrases which they associate with the word assigned to their group. Use the following as an oral example:

    LAKE: blue water, cool, wet, waves, sailboats, rippling

4. After ample time is given for completion of this exercise, allow each group to share their descriptive words by doing the following:

    a. One member of the group should write the six descriptive words or phrases on the board.

    b. All students (except those in the group whose words are on the board) should try to figure out the word being described.

    c. Once the word is known, allow others to add to the descriptive list.

Copyright © 1989, Good Apple, Inc.

GA1052

# CHAPTER 16

- At the end of Chapter 16, Pa makes a checkers game for Laura and him. Ask:

    a. Who has ever played checkers?
    b. How do you play checkers?
    c. What are Chinese checkers?
    d. Who has played Chinese checkers?
    e. How are Chinese checkers different from regular checkers?

- Have a set of regular checkers and Chinese checkers for the class to use in their spare time.

# CHAPTER 19

- In Chapter 19, all of the Christmases of the past were being talked about while the Ingalls family sat cozy and snug in their little house. Laura remembered Mr. Edwards, Ma remembered the time Pa was lost in the blizzard and Mary recalled the Christmas tree at church.

- Why do people recall Christmases past? Discuss this question in detail.

    a. Do people ever feel sad at Christmas?
    b. Do you ever feel sad at Chrstimas?
    c. What does Christmas really stand for?

# CHAPTER 21

- As usual, the Ingalls had a very Merry Christmas! Dinner was delicious, and as a surprise to all, Mr. and Mrs. Boast joined in the merriment.

- The following recipe can be found in *The Little House Cookbook*:

    Popcorn ..................................................page 215

    *By the Shores of Silver Lake* should be read around Christmas, and making popcorn can add to the festive season.

- Not only can it be eaten while you read orally, but it can be strung on quilting thread and used to decorate the class Christmas tree!

Copyright © 1989, Good Apple, Inc.

GA1052

# FACT OR OPINION?

TEACHER DIRECTIONS:

As an introduction to this game, begin with a discussion of what is a fact and what is an opinion.

Divide the class into two groups.

Explain to the class that you will be making statements based on *By the Shores of Silver Lake*. Alternate from one team to the other, giving each student a statement to which he must respond by stating fact or opinion and explaining why.

If the student answers correctly, his/her team earns a point. The team with the most points wins. Teachers may use as many statements as they like, including any or all from the examples listed.

# FACT OR OPINION?

EXAMPLES:

1. _____ Laura and Lena had fun riding the black ponies.
2. _____ Laura described things in words to Mary.
3. _____ Riding on the train is always fun.
4. _____ The Ingalls spent the winter in the surveyor's house.
5. _____ The surveyor's house was the biggest in the world!
6. _____ The Ingalls claim was on the prettiest part of the prairie.
7. _____ Pa called Laura "Flutterbudget."
8. _____ Buffalos are the biggest animals in the world.

ANSWER KEY:

1. F    5. O
2. F    6. O
3. O    7. F
4. F    8. O

Copyright © 1989, Good Apple, Inc.

GA1052

# REMEMBERING DETAILS

**TEACHER DIRECTIONS:**

This work sheet needs very little introduction. A simple question and answer period at the conclusion of the book can serve as a lead-in exercise.

Place the work sheets at a learning center. Require all students to complete one work sheet by coming to the center during his/ her free time. At the center, have a copy of *By the Shores of Silver Lake* for the children to refer to. Provide an answer key.

**ANSWER KEY:**

1. Aunt Docia
2. Storekeeper, bookkeeper, timekeeper
3. Train
4. Railroad
5. Surveyor's house
6. File on a claim
7. Surveyor came back and the claim shanty was not built.
8. Claim shanty

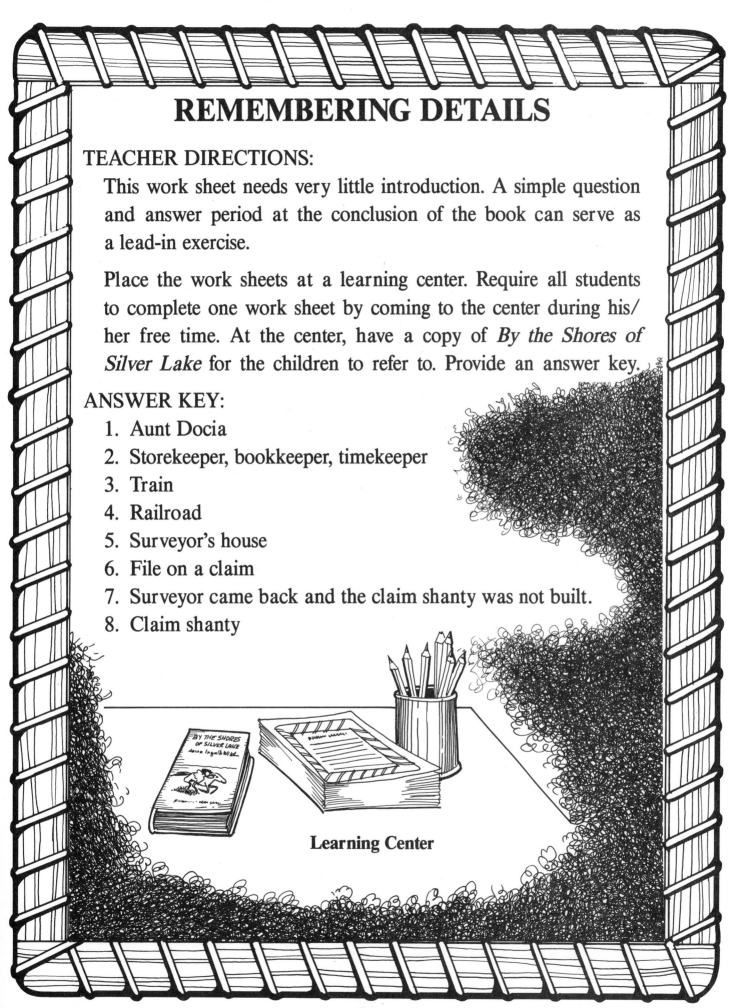

**Learning Center**

Copyright © 1989, Good Apple, Inc.

GA1052

# REMEMBERING DETAILS

Can you remember some of the important details from *By the Shores of Silver Lake*? Answer the questions below. Remember, your answers *must* be in complete sentences!

1. Who offered Pa the job on Silver Lake? _____

_____

2. What was Pa's job on Silver Lake?_____

_____

3. How did Ma, Mary, Laura, Carrie, and Grace get to Silver Lake?

_____

4. Laura and Pa had a wonderful afternoon on the prairie. Pa taught Laura how what was built? _____

_____

5. Whose house did the Ingalls family spend their first winter in?

_____

6. Pa had to hurry and do what before the spring rush?_____

_____

7. Why did the Ingalls family move to town and live in Pa's store building? _____

_____

8. What was the little house that Pa built on the homestead called?

Copyright © 1989, Good Apple, Inc.
GA1052

# UNIT 5
# THE LONG WINTER

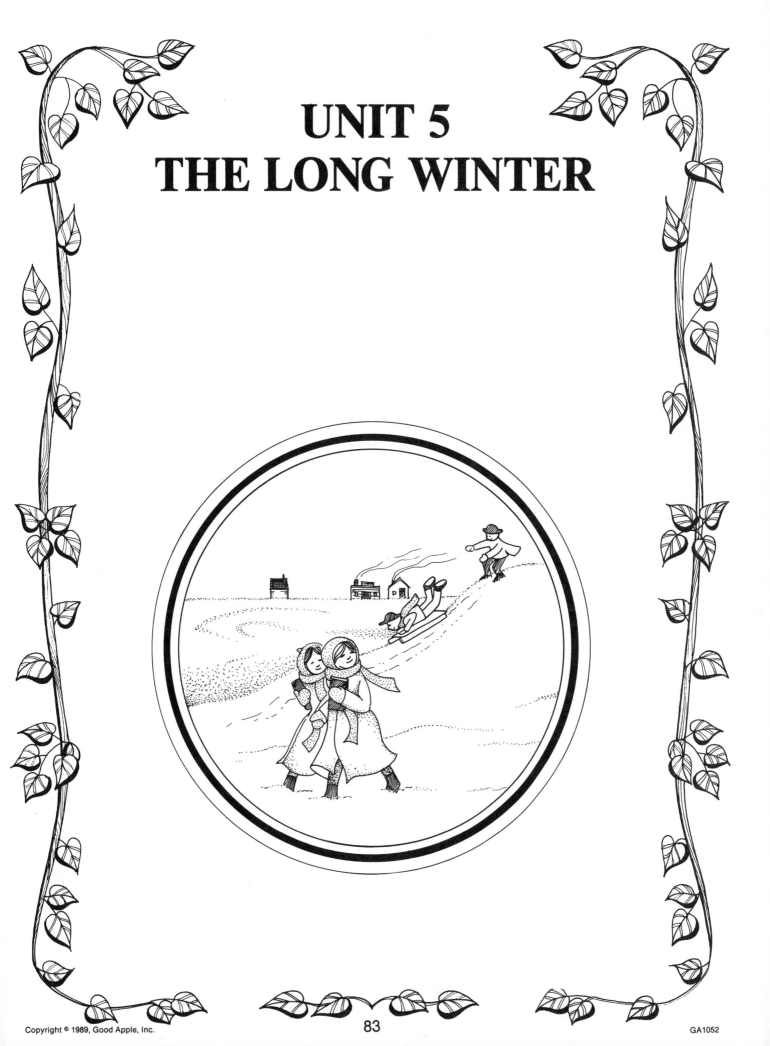

Copyright © 1989, Good Apple, Inc.

GA1052

# UNIT 5

| SKILL | ACTIVITY |
|---|---|
| Oral and Listening Skills | Entire Unit |
| Bulletin Board Idea | Snowmen |
| Following Directions | Learning Center |
| Comprehension Skills | Following Directions |
| Work Attack Skills | Syllables Game |
| Creative Skills | Journals and Individual Projects |
| Art | Snowmen |
| Social Studies | Map Skills |

Copyright © 1989, Good Apple, Inc.

GA1052

# UNIT 5
# THE LONG WINTER

Blizzard after blizzard seemed to hit the Dakota prairies, one after another, until the trains could not reach the small town of De Smet, South Dakota, with desperately needed food for the starving town. The Ingalls family, too, needed food, but their love and commitment to each other was strong and together they made it through the long hard winter. As Pa said, "It can't beat us"—and it didn't.

# STORY INTRODUCTION

This is the only one of Mrs. Wilder's books which can be depressing to the students and make them become restless while it is being read. To avoid this same restlessness year after year, approach this unit with one goal in mind: to keep students interested and *listening*! Following are some suggested activities.

Copyright © 1989, Good Apple, Inc.

GA1052

# JOURNALS

Require students to keep journals. They are to make entries after listening to you read each chapter of *The Long Winter*. They are to pretend *they* are living in the town of De Smet during the winter of 1880-1881 and are classmates of Mary and Laura!

The journal entry should include:
    Each day's date (remember it's 1880-1881)
    The day's weather
    What they did that day
    How they felt that day

## INSTRUCTIONS FOR MAKING THE JOURNAL
SUPPLIES:
    snowflake pattern
    2 pieces of blue 9″ x 11″ (23.04 x 28.16 cm) construction paper
    35 sheets of notebook paper (supplied by students)
    glue
    stapler

TEACHER DIRECTIONS:
1. Run off enough snowflakes, one for each student.
2. Have students cut out snowflakes.
3. Pass out two sheets of blue construction paper to each student.
4. Glue snowflake to one piece of construction paper.
5. Place notebook paper between both sheets of construction paper.
6. Either pass your stapler around the room and allow students to staple booklets at left side top, middle and bottom, or staple yourself.
7. Have the class write their names on the covers.

Copyright © 1989, Good Apple, Inc.

GA1052

# SNOWFLAKE PATTERN

Copyright © 1989, Good Apple, Inc.

87

GA1052

# INDIVIDUAL PROJECTS

TEACHER DIRECTIONS:

1. Read several chapters of *The Long Winter* before telling the class that they will be doing individual projects. Each student (or two working together) will be required to turn in a project based on one chapter from the book.

2. The project must be as realistic as possible (that is, no modern dress on dolls, no electric stoves, etc.)

3. Any type of project is acceptable—posters, dioramas, mobiles, homemade items. This project is to be tangible—no written paper or book reports.

4. You may receive help from your family; however this is your project. If your mother or father would like to make an item for your project (for example, a knitted purse, dress for doll, wooden bedstead), that is fine as long as it's your thought, plan and idea.

5. Answer questions the class may ask, but don't give suggestions; leave them totally on their own!

6. Set no deadline for projects, except that they must be in by the time the book is finished.

7. When you arrive at Chapters 22-24, remind students there is only one week of reading left and set a reasonable deadline for the reading time.

As projects begin to come in, they may be:

1. Displayed throughout the classroom

2. Displayed in the showcase

3. Displayed in the school Learning Resource Center (with the librarian's cooperation)

4. Shared with the younger children (with the primary teacher's permission). Students should be able to tell the youngsters about *The Long Winter* and what their projects are all about.

Copyright © 1989, Good Apple, Inc.

GA1052

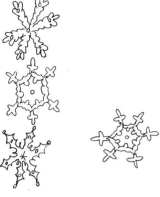

# HOW MANY SYLLABLES?

## GAME

TEACHER DIRECTIONS:
1. Laminate the words on pages 90-92 and cut out.
2. Divide the class into two teams.
3. Line up the two teams and stand between them.
4. Flash one card at a time to the first player on the two teams.
5. The team that shouts out the correct number of syllables gets a point.
6. The team with the most points wins!

# FOLLOWING DIRECTIONS

## LEARNING CENTER

TEACHER DIRECTIONS:
1. Glue the Visiting De Smet sheet (page 93) to a piece of cardboard and cover with laminating material.
2. Place at a learning center.
3. Place several grease pencils or crayons in a container at the center.
4. Require each student to go to the center and complete the game.
5. Self-check by having a key at the center.

Copyright © 1989, Good Apple, Inc.

GA1052

# HOW MANY SYLLABLES?

| | |
|---|---|
| warning | blizzard |
| supplies | secure |
| dangerous | grass |
| wheat | glittering |
| southward | handcar |

Copyright © 1989, Good Apple, Inc.

90

GA1052

# HOW MANY SYLLABLES?

| | |
|---|---|
| train | Tennessee |
| bread | thankful |
| fair | kerosene |
| errand | study |
| town | frozen |

Copyright © 1989, Good Apple, Inc.

GA1052

# HOW MANY SYLLABLES?

| | |
|---|---|
| coal | locomotive |
| lumber yard | muskrats |
| mail | snug |
| trembling | hay |
| superintendent | prairie |

Copyright © 1989, Good Apple, Inc.

GA1052

# FOLLOWING DIRECTIONS
## VISITING DE SMET

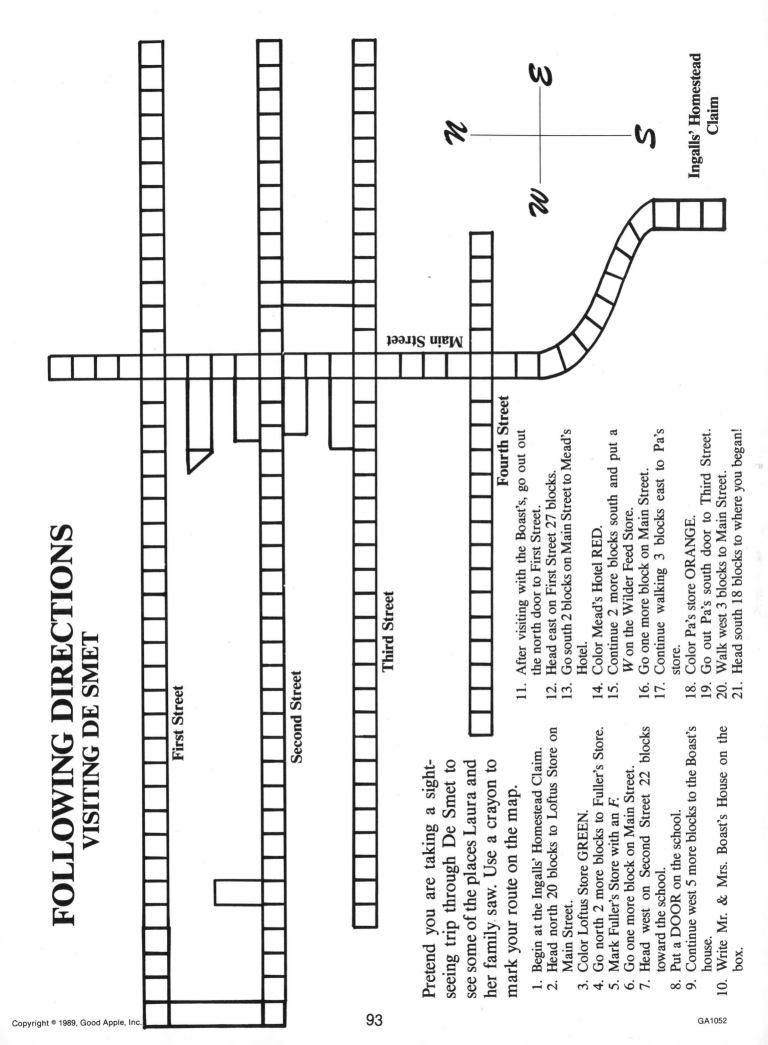

Pretend you are taking a sight-seeing trip through De Smet to see some of the places Laura and her family saw. Use a crayon to mark your route on the map.

1. Begin at the Ingalls' Homestead Claim.
2. Head north 20 blocks to Loftus Store on Main Street.
3. Color Loftus Store GREEN.
4. Go north 2 more blocks to Fuller's Store.
5. Mark Fuller's Store with an *F*.
6. Go one more block on Main Street.
7. Head west on Second Street 22 blocks toward the school.
8. Put a DOOR on the school.
9. Continue west 5 more blocks to the Boast's house.
10. Write Mr. & Mrs. Boast's House on the box.
11. After visiting with the Boast's, go out out the north door to First Street.
12. Head east on First Street 27 blocks.
13. Go south 2 blocks on Main Street to Mead's Hotel.
14. Color Mead's Hotel RED.
15. Continue 2 more blocks south and put a *W* on the Wilder Feed Store.
16. Go one more block on Main Street.
17. Continue walking 3 blocks east to Pa's store.
18. Color Pa's store ORANGE.
19. Go out Pa's south door to Third Street.
20. Walk west 3 blocks to Main Street.
21. Head south 18 blocks to where you began!

Ingalls' Homestead Claim

First Street

Second Street

Third Street

Fourth Street

Main Street

Copyright © 1989, Good Apple, Inc.

93

GA1052

# SNOWMEN

## BULLETIN BOARD

### SUPPLIES:

9″ x 11″ (23.04 cm x 28.16 cm) blue construction paper

12″ x 18″ (30.72 cm x 46.08 cm) white construction paper

glue

4″ x 4″ (10.24 cm x 10.24 cm) various colors construction paper

black construction paper scraps

### TEACHER DIRECTIONS:

1. Pass out one piece blue construction paper and one piece white construction paper to each student.
2. Allow students to choose two 4″ x 4″ (10.24 cm x 10.24 cm) pieces of colored construction paper.
3. Pass out black scraps.
4. Tell class they are making snowmen. First they should sketch a snowman with their pencils on the blue construction paper.
5. Tear or cut the white construction paper into small pieces.
6. Put a dab of glue in the middle of each piece of white paper and place on snowman (overlap pieces and place at random).
7. After all white pieces are placed (discard any leftovers), add eyes, hat, scarf and mouth.
8. Allow students to add brooms, etc., if desired.

This bulletin board may be used to display various individual projects turned in by the students.

# HELLO SNOW!

Copyright © 1989, Good Apple, Inc.

GA1052

# UNIT 6
# LITTLE TOWN ON THE PRAIRIE

Copyright © 1989, Good Apple, Inc.

GA1052

# UNIT 6

| SKILL | ACTIVITY |
|---|---|
| Oral and Listening Skills | Entire Unit |
| Writing Skills | Skit |
| Creative Skills | Skit |
| Comprehension Skills | Synonyms Work Sheet |
| Bulletin Board Idea | |

Copyright © 1989, Good Apple, Inc.

GA1052

# UNIT 6

# LITTLE TOWN ON THE PRAIRIE

De Smet, Dakota Territory—once it was a prairie where the only living thing was grass and wildlife. Now it's a growing town with stores and a church all its own. Laura, now age 15, is also growing up. Mary has gone to the school for the blind in Iowa, and Laura experiences her first job in town.

Children love this Wilder book, especially Chapters 11-16. They love the mischievous Laura because most students can relate to her! While reading this book, you will notice a greater interest on the part of your students. This comes from being able to see Laura as "naughty" at times and being able to see themselves!

*Little Town on the Prairie* still holds the magic of adventure and family togetherness so common in the Ingalls family. Laura truly begins to enjoy living among other people in town. She experiences lasting friendships from her school days and is becoming a young lady.

When the time comes to read *Little Town on the Prairie*, assign any or all of the following activities as you read the book in its entirety. The skit may be used as a culminating activity.

Copyright © 1989, Good Apple, Inc.

GA1052

# SYNONYMS

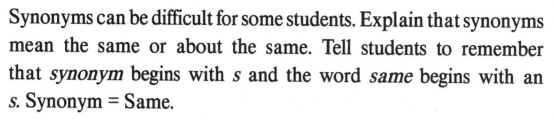

**TEACHER DIRECTIONS:**

Synonyms can be difficult for some students. Explain that synonyms mean the same or about the same. Tell students to remember that *synonym* begins with *s* and the word *same* begins with an *s*. Synonym = Same.

The work sheet on page 99 can be given after the above discussion.

**ANSWER KEY:**

| | |
|---|---|
| 1. little | 7. somber |
| 2. fast | 8. happy |
| 3. dinner | 9. gift |
| 4. home | 10. angry |
| 5. beautiful | 11. snowstorm |
| 6. bang | 12. happy |

## SIMPLE SIMON SYNONYMS

### BULLETIN BOARD

**MATERIALS NEEDED:**

1. Green border
2. Orange block letters to read "Simple Simon Synonyms"
3. 9″ x 11″ (23.04 cm x 28.16 cm) yellow construction paper for students to glue on synonyms for the activity on the following page.

Copyright © 1989, Good Apple, Inc.

GA1052

# SYNONYMS

Synonyms are words that mean the same, or nearly the same. Both Mary and Laura have trouble matching the synonyms with the words in the word list below. Will you help them? Cut out the words in the word list and glue them to a piece of yellow construction paper. Cut out each synonym and match it to a word in the word list. Glue the synonyms in place. Good luck! The students' work sheets may then be displayed on the "Simple Simon Synonyms" bulletin board.

| WORD LIST | SYNONYM |
|---|---|
| Example:     wet | damp |
| 1. tiny | dinner |
| 2. rapid | bang |
| 3. supper | happy |
| 4. house | snowstorm |
| 5. lovely | little |
| 6. boom | happy |
| 7. sober | angry |
| 8. glad | gift |
| 9. package | home |
| 10. furious | fast |
| 11. blizzard | somber |
| 12. merry | beautiful |

Copyright © 1989, Good Apple, Inc.

GA1052

# SKIT

## TEACHER DIRECTIONS:

Divide the class into groups of five. Each group will put on a skit based on two or more chapters of the book. These chapter combinations can be used or others substituted:

Chapters 2 and 8
Chapters 4, 5, 6 and 7
Chapters 11, 13, 14 and 15
Chapters 10 and 18
Chapters 24 and 25

In choosing the assignments for each group, use your formal class list and assign numbers: 1, 2, 3, 4, 5; 1, 2, 3, 4, 5. Each group assembles in a straight line. Write down the chapter numbers on five sheets of paper. The first member of each group draws a slip and thus it is decided which group will have which chapters. The groups should be given class time each day for five to seven days to prepare their skits. They can do as the group members see fit in this activity—combine parts, eliminate or add. The only other requirement is that each group has *one* writer. Each group member *must* contribute to the skit, but only one person will do the actual writing. Each group will turn in a copy of the skit to the teacher upon completion. The skits can be performed in front of the class, to other classes, or at an all-school assembly.

Copyright © 1989, Good Apple, Inc.

GA1052

# UNIT 7
# THESE HAPPY GOLDEN YEARS

Copyright © 1989, Good Apple, Inc.

GA1052

# UNIT 7

| SKILL | ACTIVITY |
| --- | --- |
| Oral and Listening Skills | Entire Unit |
| Music | Singing |
| Art | Quilt |
| Math | Quilt |
| Comprehension Skills | Work Sheet |
| Bulletin Board Idea | Quilt |

Copyright © 1989, Good Apple, Inc.

GA1052

# UNIT 7

# THESE HAPPY GOLDEN YEARS

The little town on the prairie—De Smet—was growing day by day. Laura soon found living in town a pleasure, since she had many friends with whom to keep company. Laura was growing up—and quicker than she had anticipated. At the age of fifteen, she was going away to a small town twelve miles south to teach school.

*These Happy Golden Years* explores the maturing years of Laura Ingalls. She was suddenly thrust into a situation of teaching school and living at the Brewsters, which she found almost unbearable. Laura also became attracted to Almanzo Wilder, who was ten years older.

*These Happy Golden Years* takes its readers into the settling years for the Ingalls family. The stability of a routine, happy life had finally come to them. They were happy; they were content; they were the Ingalls, whose love and compassion and determination never died.

When reading *These Happy Golden Years*, you may notice that children seem to lose interest. Their interest in Laura and her family hasn't changed, but what has is their understanding of the material being read. This particular book deals with Laura as a young girl maturing into womanhood. Her inner feelings of fear are expressed while living at the Brewsters as well as her feelings of affection for Almanzo Wilder, her future husband. Children of intermediate age are generally not acquainted with such feelings. They do not have to deal with having a job or falling in love. Taking the above into consideration, the author's intention was to create a unit which would keep in mind the age group of the children while focusing some attention on Laura's maturity. This is done through music, art and work sheets.

Copyright © 1989, Good Apple, Inc.

GA1052

# MUSIC

Pa's fiddle rang out in each "Little House" book, but music has not been used as an activity until now. After the chapters which contain songs are read, follow up each with the singing of a song. It seems an appropriate conclusion since the happiest times for Laura were when Pa would play. At the end of *These Happy Golden Years*, Laura and Almanzo are beginning what they hope will be more Golden Years and Laura is reminded of Pa's music. The following songs are from *The Laura Ingalls Wilder Songbook* by Eugenia Garson. These ten songs are sung in *These Happy Golden Years*. The first number is the page on which it can be found in *Golden Years*; the second number indicates its location in the songbook. All songs are arranged for piano and guitar. If neither is available, a tape can be made or the songs may be sung unaccompanied.

"My Sabbath Home"—p. 41; pp. 144, 145

"Polly-Wolly-Doodle"—p. 155; pp. 70, 71

"Golden Years Are Passing By"—p. 156; pp. 38, 39

"Oh, Whistle and I'll Come to You, My Lad"—p. 184; pp. 106, 107

"In the Starlight"—p. 207; pp. 100, 101, 102

"The Singing School"—p. 212; pp. 60, 61, 62

"In Dreamland Far Away"—p. 216; pp. 98, 99

"My Heart Is Sair [sic] for Somebody"—p. 226; pp. 130, 131

"Come in and Shut the Door"—p. 227; pp. 94, 95

"Love's Old Sweet Song"—p. 277; pp. 30, 31, 32

Copyright © 1989, Good Apple, Inc.

GA1052

# NINE-PATCH QUILT

## ART

**SUPPLIES:**

wrapping paper (any color or design)

12″ (30.72 cm) square white construction paper

glue

ruler

4″ (10.24 cm) square tagboard pattern

**TEACHER DIRECTIONS:**

1. Supply 12″ (30.72 cm) square white construction paper. (Children can bring wrapping paper from home.)
2. Cut out enough 4″ (10.24 cm) square tagboard patterns so each row of students has at least one block.
3. Carefully go over all student directions with the children.
4. Collect all quilt blocks.
5. Punch approximately six holes using a paper punch on each side of each quilt block.
6. Connect blocks together with yarn.
7. Display as a bulletin board entitled "Laura Ingalls Wilder Nine-Patch Quilt."

**STUDENT DIRECTIONS:**

1. Place your ruler on the white construction paper square. Measure down from the top 4″ (10.24 cm) and 8″ (25.6 cm) and in from the left side 4″ (10.24 cm) and 8″ (25.6 cm) and put dots. Then using your ruler, draw lines from top to bottom and side to side that intersect the dots (see illustration).

Copyright © 1989, Good Apple, Inc.

GA1052

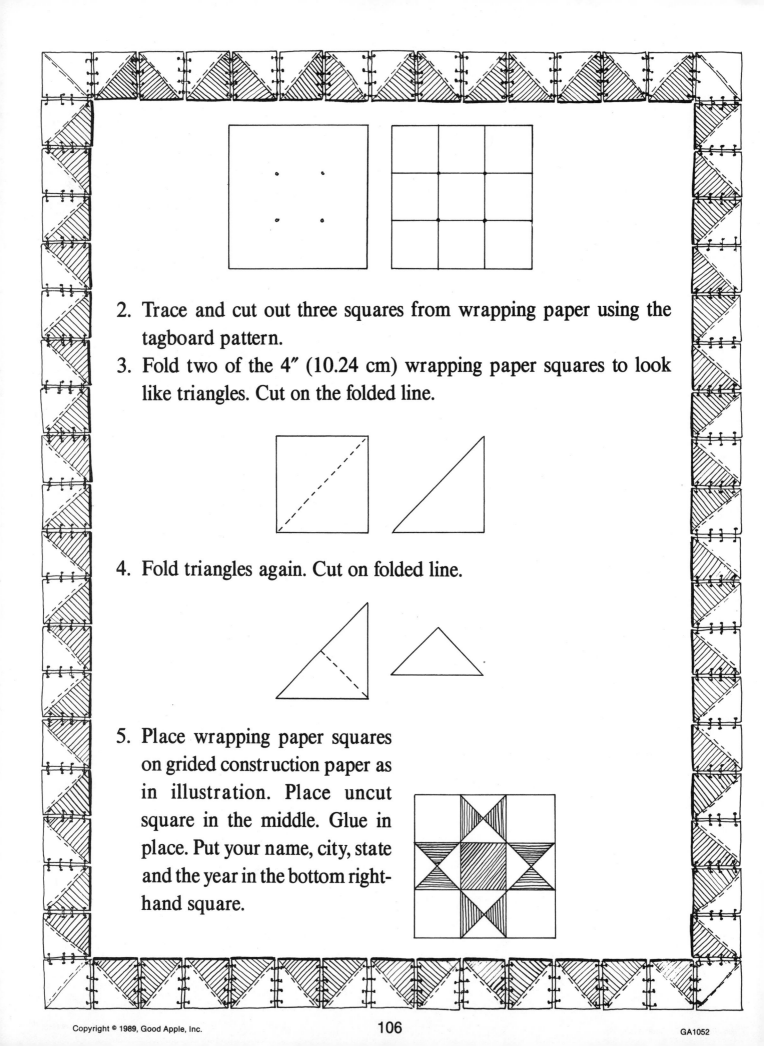

2. Trace and cut out three squares from wrapping paper using the tagboard pattern.

3. Fold two of the 4″ (10.24 cm) wrapping paper squares to look like triangles. Cut on the folded line.

4. Fold triangles again. Cut on folded line.

5. Place wrapping paper squares on grided construction paper as in illustration. Place uncut square in the middle. Glue in place. Put your name, city, state and the year in the bottom right-hand square.

Copyright © 1989, Good Apple, Inc.

GA1052

# REMEMBERING DETAILS

**TEACHER DIRECTIONS:**

This work sheet may be done in any of the following ways:

1. Make an overhead of the crossword puzzle and complete as an entire class.
2. Divide the class into groups of four and have each group complete the puzzle.
3. Pass out the puzzle for individual completion and turn in when finished.

**ANSWER KEY:**

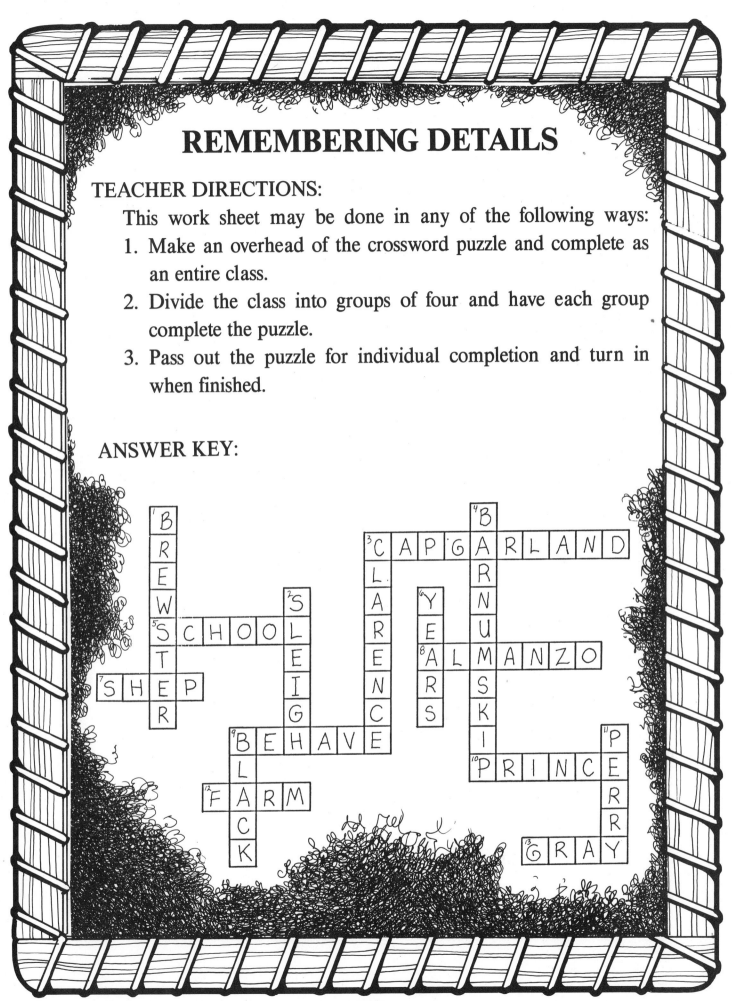

Copyright © 1989, Good Apple, Inc.

GA1052

# REMEMBERING DETAILS

Now that we have finished reading *These Happy Golden Years*, let's see what you remember!

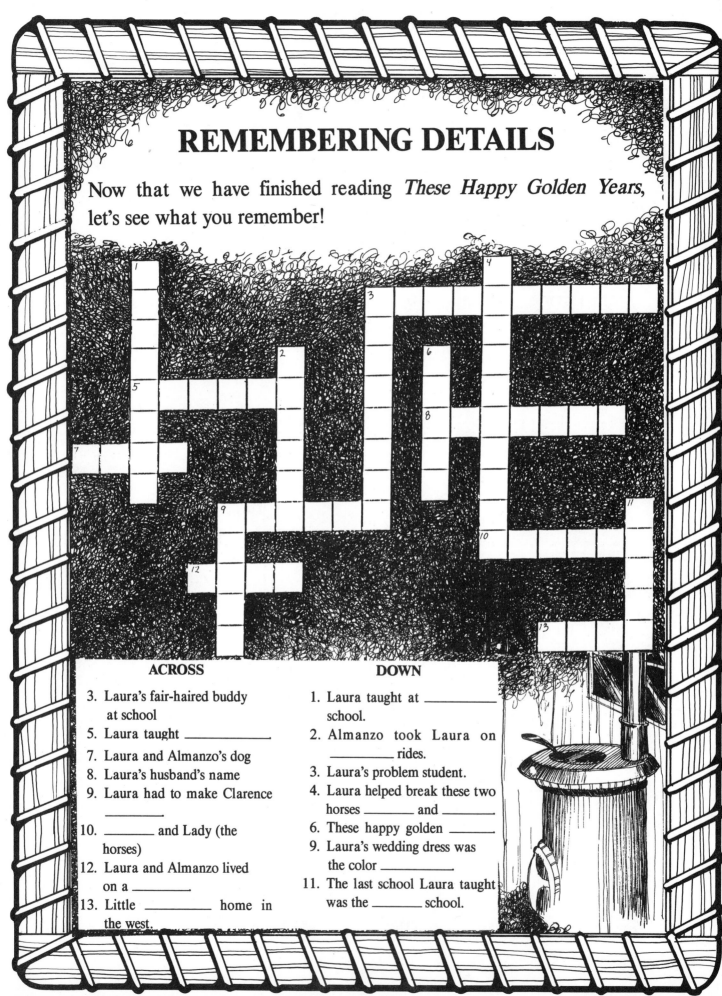

**ACROSS**

3. Laura's fair-haired buddy at school
5. Laura taught _____
7. Laura and Almanzo's dog
8. Laura's husband's name
9. Laura had to make Clarence _____
10. _____ and Lady (the horses)
12. Laura and Almanzo lived on a _____
13. Little _____ home in the west.

**DOWN**

1. Laura taught at _____ school.
2. Almanzo took Laura on _____ rides.
3. Laura's problem student.
4. Laura helped break these two horses _____ and _____
6. These happy golden _____
9. Laura's wedding dress was the color _____
11. The last school Laura taught was the _____ school.

Copyright © 1989, Good Apple, Inc.

108

GA1052

# BIBLIOGRAPHY

Anderson, William. *The Story of the Ingalls*. De Smet, South Dakota: Laura Ingalls Wilder Memorial Society, Inc., 1971.

_____. *Laura Wilder of Mansfield*. De Smet, South Dakota: Laura Ingalls Wilder Memorial Society, Inc., 1974.

Garson, Eugenia. *The Laura Ingalls Wilder Songbook*. New York: Harper & Row, 1953.

*Laura Ingalls Wilder Lore*. De Smet, South Dakota: Laura Ingalls Wilder Memorial Society, Inc., Fall-Winter 1978. (Newsletter)

Lichty, Irene V. *The Ingalls Family from Plum Creek to Walnut Grove via Burr Oak, Iowa*. Missouri: n.p., 1970.

Walker, Barbara M. *The Little House Cookbook: Frontier Foods from Laura Ingalls Wilder's Classic Stories*. New York: Harper & Row, 1979.

Wilder, Laura Ingalls. *Little House in the Big Woods*. New York: Harper & Row, 1932.

_____. *Little House on the Prairie*. New York: Harper & Row, 1935.

_____. *On the Banks of Plum Creek*. New York: Harper & Row, 1937.

_____. *By the Shores of Silver Lake*. New York: Harper & Row, 1939.

_____. *The Long Winter*. New York: Harper & Row, 1940.

_____. *Little Town on the Prairie*. New York: Harper & Row, 1941.

_____. *These Happy Golden Years*. New York: Harper & Row, 1943.

Zochert, Donald. *Laura, the Life of Laura Ingalls Wilder*. Chicago: Regnery Company, 1976.

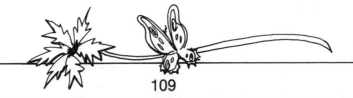

Copyright © 1989, Good Apple, Inc.
GA1052

## Where to obtain information on
## Laura Ingalls Wilder and her family:

Laura Ingalls Wilder
Memorial Society, Inc.
De Smet, South Dakota 57231

Laura Ingalls Wilder
Rose Wilder Lane Home and Museum
Mansfield, Missouri 65704

Copyright © 1989, Good Apple, Inc.

GA1052